T0253278

VOLUME 3

MÍRIAM BONASTRE TUR

CLARION BOOKS
IMPRINTS OF HARPERCOLLINSPUBLISHERS

CLARION BOOKS IS AN IMPRINT OF HARPERCOLLINS PUBLISHERS.
HARPERALLEY IS AN IMPRINT OF HARPERCOLLINS PUBLISHERS.

HOOKY VOLUME 3

ISBN 978-0-35-869358-1 — ISBN 978-0-35-869357-4 (PBK.)
ISBN 978-0-06-334183-8 (SIGNED EDITION)

LETTERING BY NATALIE FONDRIEST

PB: 23-WOZ-3
HC: 23-WOZ-2

FIRST EDITION
A DIGITAL VERSION OF *HOOKY* WAS ORIGINALLY PUBLISHED ON
WEBTOON IN 2015.

CHAPTER 58

DORIAN...
WHERE ARE YOU?
AH!
MARK!
EVANS CA
HELLO, DANI.
HAVE YOU SEEN MY BROTHER?
I NEED HELP WITH SOME HOMEWORK MASTER PENDRAGON ASSIGNED ME!
YEAH, LOOK.
DORIAN'S OVER THERE.
AH?!
DORI--!
MWAH!♥

WOAH! WHAT THE HELL ARE YOU DOING, MARK?!

I'M SORRY, I TRICKED YOU TO CATCH YOU BY SURPRISE.

YOU HAVEN'T STOPPED BY LATELY SO I MISSED Y--

KEEP YOUR HANDS OFF OF HER, YOU FILTHY PIG!

HELLO THERE NICO!

HAVE YOU SEEN DORIAN?

NO.

HAVE YOU CHECKED THE LIBRARY?

OF COURSE I'VE CHECKED THE LIBRARY!

ARGH! WHERE IS DORIAN?

IF I FLUNK THE CLASS, MY MUM'S GONNA KILL ME!

YOU KNOW, I'M ALSO QUITE GOOD AT MAGIC.

I CAN HELP YOU OUT FOR A SMALL FEE, DANI.

HELLO EVERYONE!

ARE YOU THROWING A PARTY WITHOUT ME KNOWING?

MONICA!

HOW'S THE MARRIED LIFE AT THE PALACE?

HELLO!
DAMIEN SENDS GREETINGS!
VERY GOOD, IT'S VERY CALM!
WHAT ABOUT THAT MUSTACHE, PRINCE WILLIAM...?
DANI, TELL HIM THAT IT LOOKS REALLY BAD!
HA HA HA
DO YOU LIKE IT? I MATURED A BIT.
BUT NOW THAT HE'S THE KING, HE SAYS HE WANTS TO LOOK LIKE ONE.
AWW, STOP, SILLY! YOU'RE TICKLING ME WITH YOUR MUSTACHE!
HA-HA!
I'M GLAD TO SEE YOU GETTING ALONG SO WELL, AS ALWAYS!
BY THE WAY, MONICA!
HAVE YOU SEEN DORIAN, BY ANY CHANCE?

AH, DORIAN!
I'M GLAD TO FINALLY FIND YOU!
WELL, THAT'S TOO BAD...
HUH?
WHAT...?
DON'T YOU REMEMBER...?
NONE OF THIS IS REAL.
WHAT DO YOU MEAN...?
I'M NOT REALLY HERE, DANI...
YOU SAW ME DIE.
MANY.
YEARS.
NO...
AGO.
NO...
THIS CAN'T BE...
DORIAN...?

NICO...

YOU'RE BACK.
OF COURSE I AM, DANI...
YOU KNOW I ALWAYS COME BACK.
I BROUGHT YOU A GIFT...

HERE, DANI.

TRY THIS, IT MIGHT TRIGGER SOME MEMORIES.

...

DANI...

PLEASE...

JUST A BITE!

YOUR MAJESTY?

MARK SAID YOU USED TO ENJOY IT.

...WHO?

...YOU SERIOUSLY DON'T REMEMBER?

...

I DON'T KNOW WHAT ELSE TO DO...

I'VE ASKED MYSELF IF YOU COULD HEAR ME FOR QUITE SOME TIME--

EVEN IF I'M BY YOUR SIDE, EVEN IF I SCREAM, I'M NOT EVEN SURE IF MY VOICE ACTUALLY REACHES YOU.

...
I'D LIKE YOU TO GET OUT OF THIS PALACE, TO SHOW YOU WHAT'S GOING ON OUTSIDE.
I KNOW DEEP INSIDE YOU ARE STILL A GOOD PERSON.
SEEING WHAT'S HAPPENING IN THE WORLD RIGHT NOW... I THINK IT'D HELP YOU REACT.
...
DANI, FOR GOD'S SAKE, AT LEAST SAY SOMETHING!!
TELL ME WHAT I NEED TO DO AND I'LL DO IT RIGHT AWAY!!

AAARGH!!

UH...

WHY WERE YOU OUTSIDE FOR SO LONG, NICO?

SO LONG? I WAS ONLY GONE FOR A COUPLE OF DAYS...

YOU THINK I DON'T KNOW WHY YOU ALWAYS COME BACK, AGAIN AND AGAIN?

IT'S BECAUSE YOU CAN ONLY BE NORMAL BY MY SIDE. I SHOULD MAKE YOU PERMANENTLY TINY TO TEST YOUR LOYALTY.

WHAT ARE YOU SAYING?

I TOLD YOU A LONG TIME AGO, DANI, I'LL ALWAYS BE BY YOUR SIDE! BUT THAT DOESN'T MEAN I AGREE WITH EVERYTHING YOU DO.

IT MEANS THAT I'LL DO EVERYTHING I CAN TO MAKE YOU FEEL MORE LIKE YOUR OLD SELF.

GET OUT OF MY SIGHT.

BUT DANI, WHAT...?

DON'T CALL ME DANI. I'M YOUR QUEEN.

EVEN IF IT PAINS YOU TO ADMIT THAT, BECAUSE I KNOW YOU ONLY WISH TO SEE ALL WITCHES FALL,

TO SEE OUR KIND MARGINALIZED AND MURDERED. I WON'T ALLOW IT.

...SEE YOU SOON.

LISTEN, GIRL...

DON'T GET RID OF HIM YET.

WHY?

HE COULD BE USEFUL TO US IN THE FUTURE.

MOREOVER, YOUR DESPAIR IS DELICIOUS.

WE ALL GATHER HERE TO PAY TRIBUTE TO OUR BELOVED KING,
WHO LEFT US AFTER A LONG, PEACEFUL AND PROSPEROUS REIGN.
WE'RE DEEPLY SADDENED BY HIS LOSS,
YET THANKFUL FOR HIS KINDNESS AND FORTITUDE,
AND FOR PROTECTING US DURING THE YEARS OF THOSE EVIL WITCHES.
WE ALL ARE:
HIS SUBJECTS,
HIS GRIEVING WIFE,
THE PRINCE HEIR.
AND AFTER A LONG LIFE
I WISH IT HADN'T BEEN THAT LONG.
AND DYING PEACEFULLY SURROUNDED BY HIS LOVED ONES,
I SHOULD HAVE TAKEN CARE OF IT, AND IT WOULDN'T HAVE BEEN AS PEACEFUL.

WITH GREAT SADNESS WE SAY GOODBYE.
BUT WHAT CAN WE DO? THIS NEEDS TO BE DONE FOR YOU, WILLIAM.
HU-HU.
HUH?!
MONICA, PLEASE!! WE'RE ATTENDING A FUNERAL, TRY TO CONCEAL YOURSELF A LITTLE!!
THEY WILL FIND OUT!!
I'M SORRY, DAMIEN.
I CAN'T HELP IT. IT WAS ABOUT TIME.
OUR TIME HAS COME.

I KNOW MY FATHER WASN'T EXACTLY THE BEST PERSON IN THIS WORLD, AND DEFINITELY NOT SOMEONE YOU WERE FOND OF,
BUT YOU CAN'T JUST BURST OUT LAUGHING IN THE MIDDLE OF A FUNERAL...
I WASN'T LAUGHING AT THAT, WILL!
WELL, I COULDN'T STAND HIM, AND HE COULDN'T STAND ME EITHER.
HE NEVER FORGAVE ME FOR REFUSING TO MARRY YOU AFTER I INSISTED FOR SUCH A LONG TIME.
COME, FOLLOW ME, AND DON'T MAKE A NOISE.
NOBODY SAW WHAT YOU'RE ABOUT TO SEE.
I DID.
WELL, YOU DON'T COUNT 'CAUSE YOU WERE SPYING ON ME, NOSY.
WHOA!

I'VE BEEN WORKING ON THIS SINCE WE GOT HERE, THREE YEARS AGO.

I COULDN'T STAND THE IDEA OF BEING LOCKED INSIDE THE CASTLE, EVEN IF IT WAS FOR MY OWN SAFETY, WHILE OUTSIDE THE BATTLE WAS RAGING.

I WANTED TO GET OUT AND FIGHT, BUT I REALIZED I COULDN'T JUST GO THERE EMPTY-HANDED.

I NEEDED A PLAN.

I NEEDED TO BECOME STRONGER.

AND SO, I TRIED TO FIND INFORMATION ABOUT MAGIC.

IT WAS HARD, SINCE YOUR FATHER FORBADE ANYTHING RELATED TO WITCHCRAFT YEARS AGO.

BUT THANKS TO MY PERSUASIVE SKILLS, I GOT SOME PEOPLE TO BRING ME BOOKS FROM OTHER LOCATIONS.

DAMIEN?
YES.
MONICA...
YOU'RE...
I'VE READ, I'VE STUDIED, I'VE LEARNED.
NOW I KNOW I'M STRONGER.
AND I'VE GOT A PLAN.
ARE YOU A WITCH?!

I CAN FLY ON A BROOM AND I'M PRETTY GOOD AT MAKING POTIONS.
BUT THIS IS SO DANGEROUS, MONICA!
I KNOW.
THAT'S WHY I WAITED UNTIL YOUR FATHER WAS GONE TO PUT MY PLAN INTO ACTION.
AND THAT'S WHERE I NEED YOU, WILL.
I NEED YOU TO MARRY ME!

I THOUGHT YOU DIDN'T WANT TO MARRY ME!

CALM DOWN, MONICA.

YOU HAVE TO DO THIS.

THUMP THUMP

HE'S NOT COMING BACK ANYWAY.

HE LEFT.

SINCE THEN, THINGS HAVE GOTTEN WORSE.

HE SAID HE'D BE BACK SOON.

THERE WAS A BIG FIGHT BETWEEN THE SORCERERS AND KING EDGAR'S SOLDIERS.

THAT WAS THE LAST TIME I SAW DORIAN.

MANY DIED, BUT DANI AND HER MOTHER FLED BEFORE I COULD SEE HER AND TELL HER WHAT HAD REALLY HAPPENED.

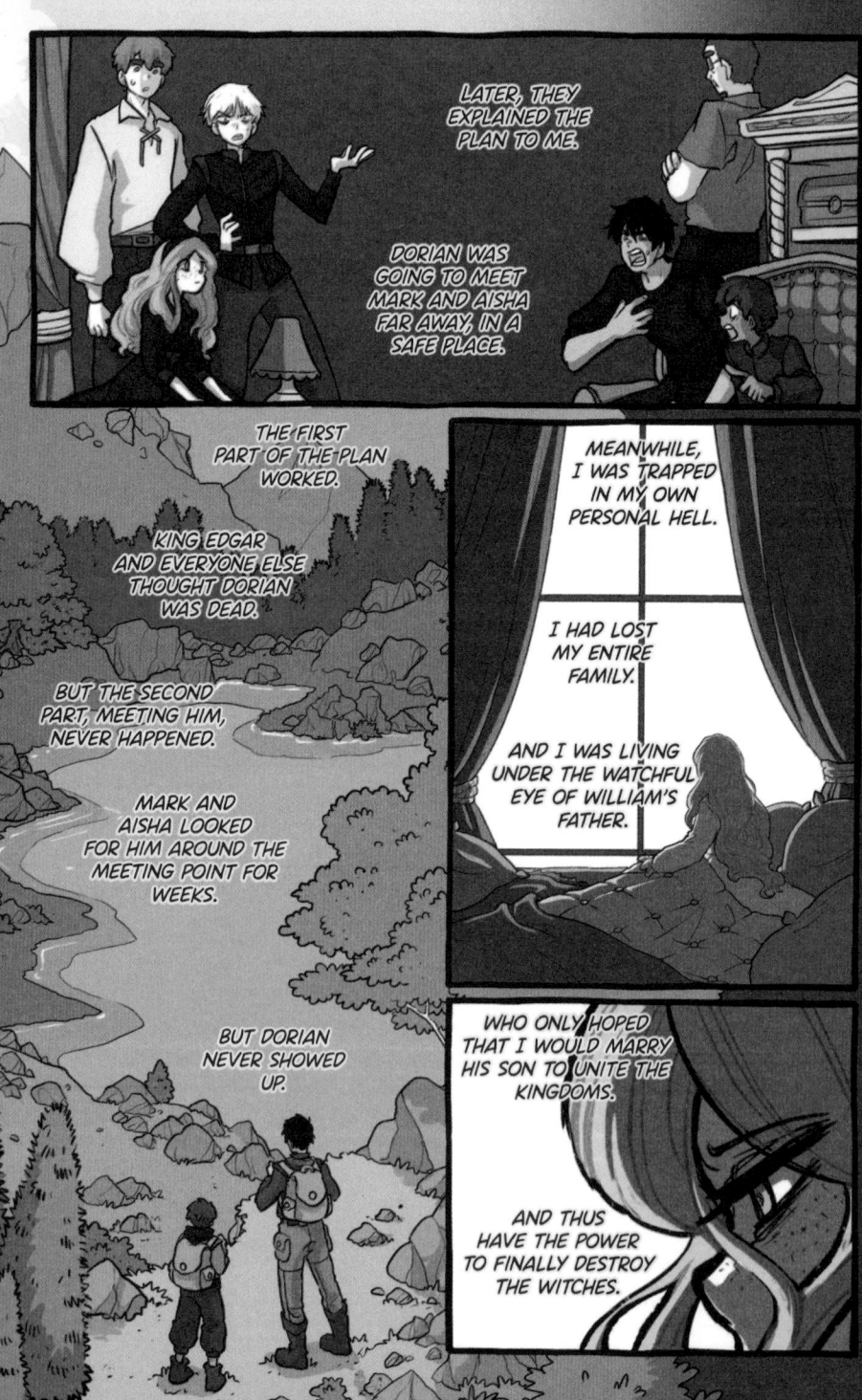

LATER, THEY EXPLAINED THE PLAN TO ME.

DORIAN WAS GOING TO MEET MARK AND AISHA FAR AWAY, IN A SAFE PLACE.

THE FIRST PART OF THE PLAN WORKED.

KING EDGAR AND EVERYONE ELSE THOUGHT DORIAN WAS DEAD.

BUT THE SECOND PART, MEETING HIM, NEVER HAPPENED.

MARK AND AISHA LOOKED FOR HIM AROUND THE MEETING POINT FOR WEEKS.

BUT DORIAN NEVER SHOWED UP.

MEANWHILE, I WAS TRAPPED IN MY OWN PERSONAL HELL.

I HAD LOST MY ENTIRE FAMILY.

AND I WAS LIVING UNDER THE WATCHFUL EYE OF WILLIAM'S FATHER.

WHO ONLY HOPED THAT I WOULD MARRY HIS SON TO UNITE THE KINGDOMS.

AND THUS HAVE THE POWER TO FINALLY DESTROY THE WITCHES.

NICO SNEAKED OUT AS OFTEN AS HE COULD

GIVING US UPDATES ABOUT DANI AND ASKING FOR HELP.

BUT WE COULDN'T GET CLOSE TO HER.

EVERY TIME THE KING SENT A MESSENGER OR A SPY, THEY ENDED UP BURNED AT THE GATES OF THE CITY.

I WANTED TO DO SOMETHING TO SAVE DANI.

AT A CERTAIN POINT, I DECIDED TO ACT.

I RESEARCHED, PRACTICED, AND BECAME STRONGER.

MARRYING WILLIAM IS ESSENTIAL TO SECURE THE SUPPORT OF THE NOBILITY AND THE PEOPLE

AND TO OBTAIN THE FULL STRENGTH OF THE ARMIES OF BOTH KINGDOMS.

THE PROMISE OF LOVE I MADE TO DORIAN

HAS FALLEN SO FAR BEHIND ME IN TIME THAT IT NOW SEEMS LIKE CHILD'S PLAY.

IT HAS BEEN THREE YEARS SINCE HE LEFT

AND MY MEMORIES OF THAT TIME HAVE SLOWLY FADED.

AFTER ALL, I ONLY SPENT ONE YEAR OF MY LIFE WITH DORIAN.

I DON'T EVEN KNOW ANYMORE WHAT PART OF HIM IS REAL...

...AND WHAT PART IS JUST AN IDEALIZED MEMORY.

EVEN THOUGH...

SOMETIMES I STILL DREAM ABOUT HIM

ABOUT TALKING AND LAUGHING TOGETHER

AND WHEN I WAKE UP, I FEEL VERY LONELY.

MONICA?

I THOUGHT YOU DIDN'T WANT TO MARRY ME!

YOU SAID NO EVERY SINGLE TIME MY FATHER MENTIONED IT!

IF I HAD MARRIED YOU, YOUR FATHER WOULD'VE USED THAT AS AN EXCUSE TO CLAIM MY FATHER'S KINGDOM!

HE WOULD'VE ENTERED IT WITH HIS ARMY TO KILL ALL THE WITCHES!

HE WOULD'VE HARMED DANI AS WELL AS OTHER INNOCENTS.

I WILL DEFEAT THE QUEEN, DANI, BUT I WANNA DO IT MY OWN WAY.

DO YOU THINK YOU CAN HEAL HER?

I HOPE SO.

THIS HAS BEEN THE MAIN FOCUS OF MY STUDIES. AN ANTIDOTE FOR DANI.

I KNOW.

PERFECT, THEN!
I'LL TELL YOU MY PLAN IN MORE DETAIL, WILL, BUT FIRST...
WE HAVE A WEDDING TO PLAN! WE'RE GETTING MARRIED IN TWO WEEKS!
LOOKS LIKE I'M FINALLY GETTING MARRIED, DAMIEN!
CONGRATULATIONS...?
EVEN THOUGH I DON'T THINK I'LL BE ABLE TO ATTEND YOUR WEDDING.
WHAAAAT?! WHY IS THAT?! YOU MUST BE THERE!
THE THING IS... TOMORROW I'LL LEAVE AGAIN WITH MARK AND AISHA.
IT LOOKS LIKE WE MIGHT BE ABLE TO FIND DORIAN THIS TIME.
WHAT? WHY DO YOU THINK THIS TIME WILL BE DIFFERENT?
AISHA TOLD ME THAT THEY RECEIVED A VISIT FROM SOMEONE WE CAN TRUST.
AND THEY BROUGHT A SIGNIFICANT CLUE.

CHAPTER 60

ALL RIGHT, THIS WAY...

DID YOU MANAGE TO FIND MILK, MARK?

NOT YET, MR. LOPEZ.

SOME THINGS ARE JUST IMPOSSIBLE TO FIND.

TRADERS DON'T COME HERE THAT OFTEN ANYMORE.

DESPITE THAT, WE BROUGHT A LOT OF FRUIT.

AWESOME!

WE'VE GOT RICE AND LENTILS, BUT ALSO SOME POTATOES AND CARROTS LEFT.

CAREFUL, LIKE SO...

OH NO, IT BROKE!

YOU NEED TO BE VERY GENTLE WHEN YOU REMOVE THE MOLD!

IF YOU'RE NOT PATIENT, YOU'LL NEVER BE ABLE TO MAKE ONE OF OUR FAMOUS EVANS-CAFÉ-STYLE APPLE PIES!

BUT IT CAN STILL BE EATEN, RIGHT?!

I DON'T THINK PEOPLE WILL MIND IF IT'S A BIT CRUMBLED...!

AH!

PENDRAGON, MY OLD FRIEND!

HELLO, EVANS.

I'M SORRY I VANISHED LIKE THAT... I KNOW YOU ALL NEEDED ME...

THE ONLY THING THAT MATTERS IS THAT YOU'RE OK. WE THOUGHT YOU WERE DEAD!

I DIDN'T COME BACK FOR PLEASURE, THERE'S STILL SOMETHING I NEED TO DO...

I CAN'T HIDE THIS ANYMORE...

MY GUILTY CONSCIENCE DOESN'T EVEN ALLOW ME TO SLEEP...
EH? WHAT ARE YOU TALKING ABOUT, PENDRAGON?
I...DID SOMETHING TERRIBLE, MY FRIEND...
IT'S ABOUT DORIAN...
TELL THE KIDS, TELL EVERYBODY... THEY SHOULD STOP LOOKING FOR HIM.
THEY'LL NEVER FIND HIM.
I DID SOMETHING TERRIBLE... I...
POW
WHO'S THERE?!
MARK!! ARE YOU OK?!
UGH...
I'M FINE... DON'T WORRY...
ONLY AN OLD ACQUAINTANCE.
CARLO?!

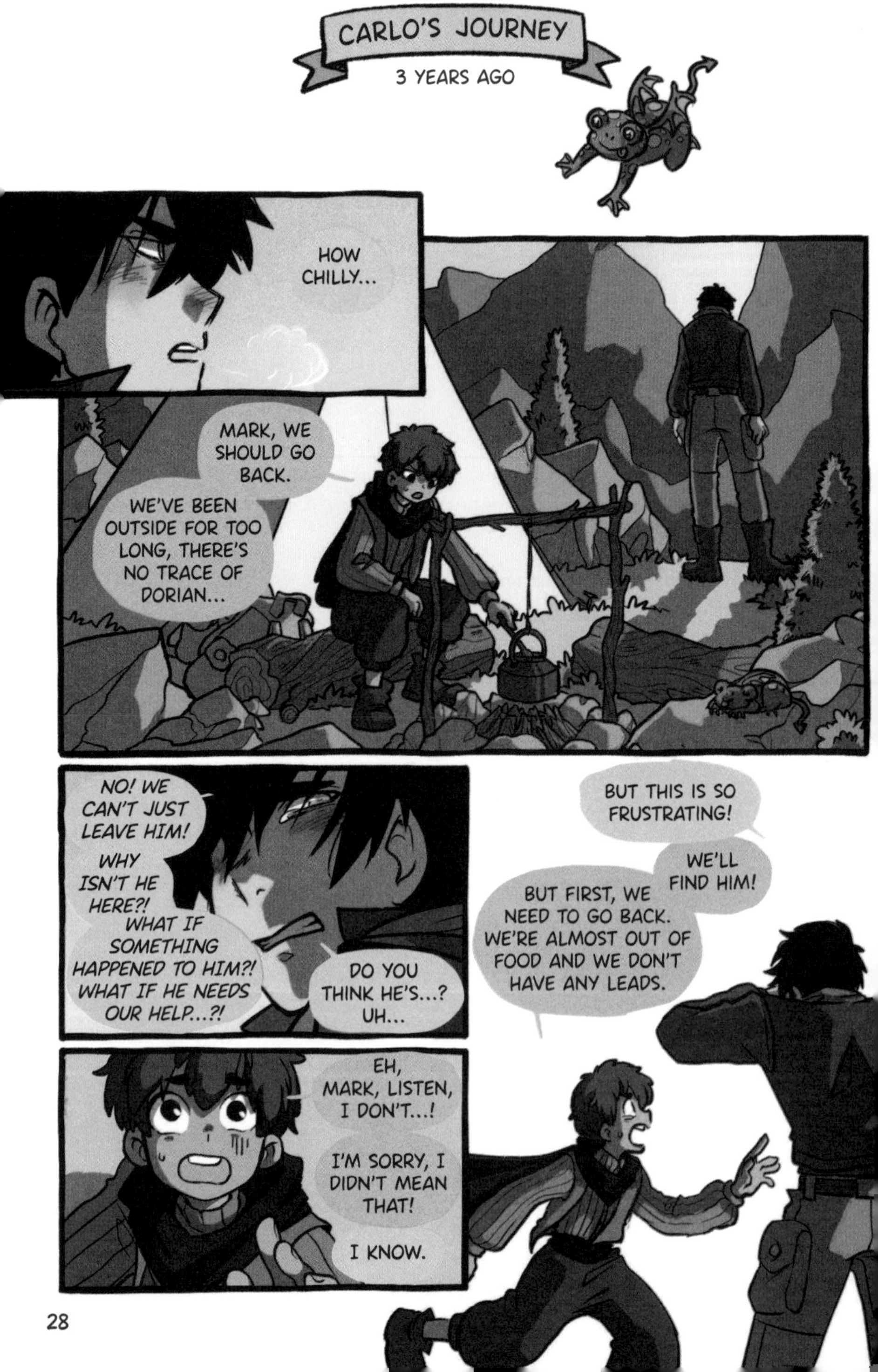
CARLO'S JOURNEY
3 YEARS AGO
HOW CHILLY...
MARK, WE SHOULD GO BACK.
WE'VE BEEN OUTSIDE FOR TOO LONG, THERE'S NO TRACE OF DORIAN...
NO! WE CAN'T JUST LEAVE HIM!
WHY ISN'T HE HERE?!
WHAT IF SOMETHING HAPPENED TO HIM?! WHAT IF HE NEEDS OUR HELP...?!
DO YOU THINK HE'S...? UH...
BUT THIS IS SO FRUSTRATING!
WE'LL FIND HIM!
BUT FIRST, WE NEED TO GO BACK. WE'RE ALMOST OUT OF FOOD AND WE DON'T HAVE ANY LEADS.
EH, MARK, LISTEN, I DON'T...!
I'M SORRY, I DIDN'T MEAN THAT!
I KNOW.

WHO KNOWS, PERHAPS HE HAS ALREADY RESCUED DANI AND THEY'RE BOTH SAFE, AT HOME.

DO YOU THINK SO...?

I DON'T KNOW.

BUT WE NEED TO LEAVE.

...ALL RIGHT THEN.

COME ON, CARLO, LET'S GET GOING!

WE SHOULD PROBABLY GO TO THE CAFÉ...

OH! WILL I MEET YOUR FATHER THEN?

DOES HE LOOK LIKE YOU, MARK?

HE'S MORE MUSCULAR, BUT YE....

AAAARGH!!

LET GO, CARLO!

WHAT IS GOING ON WITH YOU?!

LET GOOO!

...

HEY CARLO, BEHAVE! YOU MUST UNDERSTAND THAT WE CAN'T FIND DORIAN IN THESE CONDITIONS!

SO DON'T BE SILLY AND BEHAVE! ALL RIGHT?

DON'T TALK TO HIM LIKE THAT!

ALL RIGHT YOU SILLY FROG, GO AWAY!

WE DON'T NEED YOU!

CARLO, COME BACK!

CARLO!

31

CHAPTER 61

HE'S NOT.

... HOW DO YOU KNOW?

IF HE HAD DIED THREE YEARS AGO, HE'D ONLY BE A PILE OF BONES NOW.

BUT AS FAR AS WE CAN SEE, HIS BODY IS STILL INTACT.

HE MUST BE UNDER SOME SORT OF SPELL, OR IN A COMA...

I KNOW IT WANTS TO PROTECT HIM, THAT'S WHY IT DOESN'T LET US GET CLOSE TO HIM.

I WONDER IF A KISS COULD WAKE HIM UP, JUST LIKE WILLIAM?

THE PROBLEM IS HIS DRAGON.

BUT DON'T WORRY, I KNOW HOW WE'LL GET DORIAN OUT OF THERE.

AH, I THINK I CAN HELP WITH THAT.

EH?

I'LL DEFEAT THAT DRAGON!

IT'S NOT THE FIRST TIME I FACED ONE!

I'M COMING WITH YOU! WE'LL BEAT IT UP!

NO, WAIT.

AISHA.

NOT A CHANCE!

HOLD IT THERE!

POW

ARGH!

UGH...

YOU'RE REALLY DUMB, MARK. NOBODY NEEDS TO DIRECTLY FACE THE DRAGON.

ALL RIGHT, DAMIEN...

WE'LL USE THE DUMMY AS A BAIT. AS SOON AS IT GETS DISTRACTED, WE'LL GIVE DORIAN THE ANTIDOTE!

IN ORDER TO GET THE ANTIDOTE, WE MUST FIGURE OUT THE TYPE OF VENOM...

ISN'T THAT RIGHT, PENDRAGON?

... HE'S DEAD, GUYS.

I'M SORRY, BUT YOU MUST ACCEPT THAT.

DID YOU FIND ANYTHING, DAMIEN?

I'M LOOKING THROUGH MONICA'S STUDIES ON POTIONS.

THEY ARE VERY THOROUGH,

BUT I CAN'T FIND ANY ANTIDOTE TO THE POISON MASTER PENDRAGON GAVE DORIAN.

SO, I CHOSE A GENERAL HEALING POTION.

BUT, MONICA HIGHLIGHTED THIS PARTICULAR RECIPE.

SHE EVEN ADDED A LOT OF EXCLAMATION MARKS AND LITTLE STARS.

IT'S USED TO HEAL MINOR SPELLS, DIFFERENT TYPES OF WOUNDS...

HOW'S IT GOING?

DON'T MAKE HIM NERVOUS, IT'S A DELICATE MOMENT.

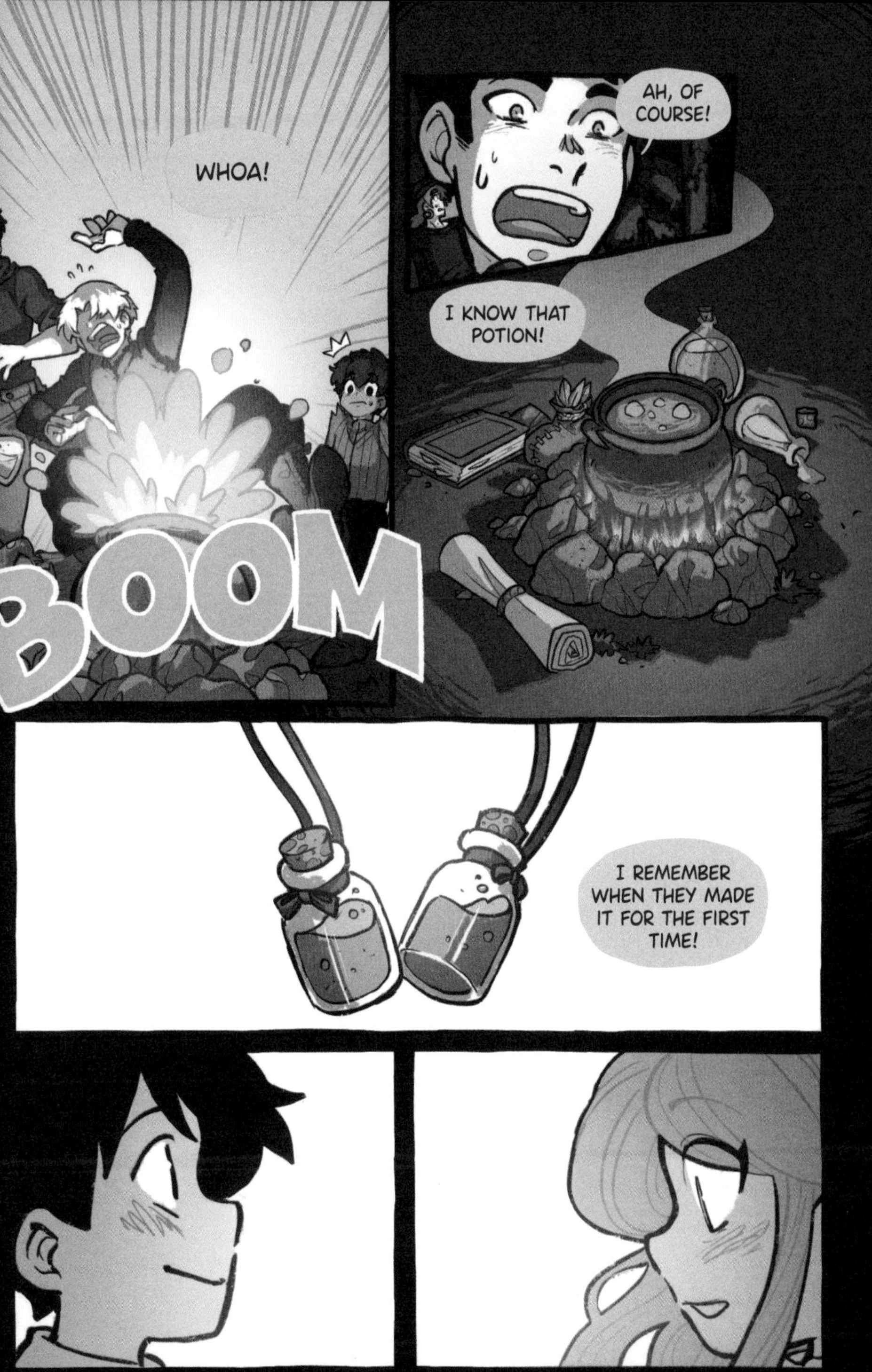
WHOA!
BOOM
AH, OF COURSE!
I KNOW THAT POTION!
I REMEMBER WHEN THEY MADE IT FOR THE FIRST TIME!

THIS WILL WORK...
HIDE BETWEEN THE TREES, DON'T LET IT SEE YOU.
AND DON'T GET TOO CLOSE, WAIT FOR THE DUMMY TO CATCH ITS ATTENTION.
HAVE YOU ALL GOT YOUR POTIONS READY?
ALL RIGHT!
COME ON, DUMMY, DO YOUR THING.
YES!
WE'RE READY!
GOOD...
WE'LL SURROUND THE DRAGON...
IT SAW THE DUMMY!
IT IS GETTING NERVOUS!
SPLIT UP, QUICKLY!
WHOEVER GETS THE OPPORTUNITY FIRST SHOULD GIVE DORIAN THE POTION.
WE NEED TO HURRY!

THE DUMMY DODGED IT!
UH...
THIS IS MY CHANCE!
DORIAN!
HERE, DRINK THIS.

HE DID IT!
AWESOME!
WELL DONE, DAMIEN.
AH...
CHOMP
CHOMP
IT...
... IT ATE THE DUMMY.
OH.
UH...
CRAP!
WE NEED TO GET OUT OF HERE!!
DORIAN, WAKE UP!

WHOA!

GUYS, GET READY TO ESCAPE!

I'LL TRY TO DISTRACT THE DRAGON, BUT WE MUST GET DORIAN OUT OF HERE...!

UH...?

IT SMELLS LIKE...

SMOKE?

AAAAAAAAARGH!

I'VE GOT YOU, DORIAN!!

POW
WATCH OUT, DAMIEN!
BEHIND YOU!
WHERE'S DORIAN...?
I MANAGED TO SHIELD THE BOTH OF US...
OH, CRAP!
COME ON,

CALM DOWN, LITTLE DRAGON...
I KNOW YOU'RE SCARED...
BUT DON'T BURN MY BROTHER!
THERE, THERE...
I'M HERE NOW.
AH...
DORIAN?
UGH...
IS THAT REALLY HIM...?
UH... I FEEL DIZZY...
DORIAN, YOU'RE ALIVE!!
THANK GOODNESS!!
I'M SO GLAD TO SEE YOU!!
I'M SO RELIEVED...!
IT LOOKS LIKE THE POTION WORKED!
ALTHOUGH HE...
WHERE AM I...?
WHERE IS DA...?
AH, HI GUYS!
AH...
AAAARGH!
UH...
DORIAN, YOU...!
UH...

I'M SO GLAD TO SEE YOU!

WHAT ARE YOU ALL DOING HERE? YOU LOOK WEIRD...

WHAT THE HELL ARE YOU SAYING, YOU'RE THE ONE LOOKING WEIRD HERE!!

YOU LOOK HORRIBLE!!

NICO, CALM DOWN...

ALTHOUGH HE DOES INDEED LOOK DREADFUL.

IT'S SO CREEPY, YOU LOOK LIKE A CORPSE!!

INCREDIBLE... I DIDN'T THINK WE'D FIND HIM...

WHAT ARE YOU TALKING ABOUT!

YOU'VE NEVER LOST HOPE, MARK!

EVEN THOUGH, "ALIVE"...

I DON'T REALLY KNOW IF HE'S THAT ALIVE...

UH...

UGH...

DORIAN!!

AH!

49

ARE YOU OK?!

YES, IT'S JUST... I FEEL REALLY WEAK...

MH?

OH... MARK...

YOU'VE CHANGED... YOU...

YOU'VE SHRUNK, RIGHT?

HA?

CAN'T YOU SEE WHAT HAPPENED HERE?!

DON'T YOU REMEMBER ANYTHING AT ALL...?!

I... WELL...

IT'S BLURRY...

AH... DAD...

MY DAD IS...

UH, AND MONICA...

UGH... MY STOMACH...

BRING HIM SOME WATER, HURRY UP.

YES!

AND... SOMETHING ELSE...

AH!

DANI! I WAS GONNA LOOK FOR DANI!

HURRY UP, WE NEED TO RESCUE HER, SHE'S BEEN WITH MY MOTHER FOR TOO MANY DAYS!!

HEH... DAYS...
YOU'VE GOT A LOT TO PROCESS, AND IT MIGHT BE HARD...
DORIAN, YOU'D BETTER SIT DOWN...
AH, MASTER PENDRAGON!
LISTEN, I THINK THE POTION YOU GAVE ME YESTERDAY WASN'T THE RIGHT ONE FOR ME...
DORIAN, WAIT.
YEAH...
I SEE...
HERE, DRINK THIS.
AND LET'S GET OUT OF HERE AS SOON AS WE CAN.
WE NEED TO KEEP HIM SAFE.
ARGH!! THE DRAGON!!

IT WON'T LET US GET AWAY WITH DORIAN!
HE'S ITS PREY!
DON'T WORRY, EVERYTHING IS UNDER CONTROL.
NO!
STOP!
?
I'M NOT HIS PREY!
HE BELIEVES I'M HIS MOM.
ISN'T THAT TRUE, LITTLE FELLA?
HE DOESN'T WANT TO SEPARATE FROM ME...
BUT I CAN'T TAKE YOU WITH ME, LITTLE ONE.
LITTLE ONE, HE SAYS...
...
OH.
WHAT ABOUT MY WAND?
WHERE'S MY WAND?
AH!
HERE IT IS!

BUT IT'S BEAUTIFUL...
?
WHAT IS HE GONNA DO?
I DON'T KNOW...
HEE-HEE!

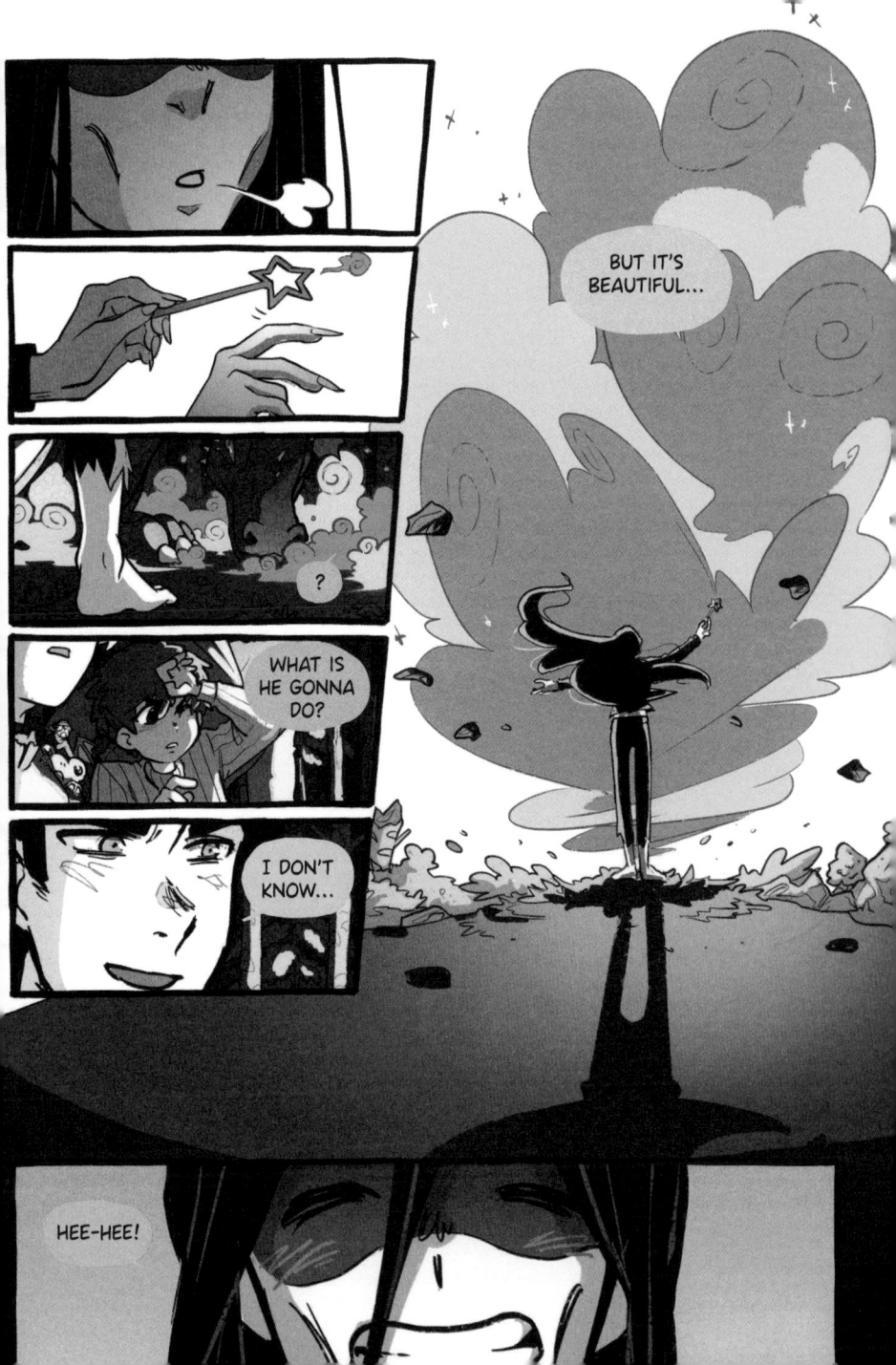

THIS WAY HE CAN JOIN US.
OH, HOW CUTE! YOU SHOULD GIVE THE LITTLE DRAGON A NAME!
YOU WANTED TO KILL IT A FEW MINUTES AGO, AISHA.
LOOK, CARLO'S ABOUT TO CRUSH HIM NOW!
HEY GUYS, CALM DOWN!
HA HA HA HA HA HA HA HA HA HA HA HA
DORIAN!
HURRY UP, HELP ME LIFT HIM!
OH...

CHAPTER 62

MAGIC? THAT'S HOW CURSES WORK.

PRINCE WILLIAM WAS ALSO IN A DEEP SLUMBER FOR MONTHS AND HE DIDN'T STARVE TO DEATH.

RIGHT, BUT DORIAN GREW UP...

LOOK AT HIM, HE'S TALLER, HE GOT BIGGER. HE MUST HAVE EATEN SOMETHING.

DO YOU WANT ME TO CARRY DORIAN FOR A BIT, MARK?

NO, DON'T WORRY, HE WEIGHS PRACTICALLY NOTHING.

YES, HE'S SO THIN... YOU CAN CLEARLY SEE HE HASN'T EATEN IN YEARS.

HOW CAN HE POSSIBLY BE ALIVE, THEN?

I BET THE DRAGON WAS TAKING CARE OF HIM. GIVING HIM REGURGITATED FOOD!

JUST LIKE MOTHER BIRDS WHEN THEY FEED THEIR BABIES!

AISHA...

NO... IT WAS MAGIC, WASN'T IT?

YUCK...

OH, WOW.

THE BRIDGE COLLAPSED.

EH!

HEY!

NO, ABSOLUTELY NOT!

DON'T YOU DARE BURY A CORPSE UNDER THIS BRIDGE!

IF YOU MESSED UP, DEAL WITH IT ON YOUR OWN, WE'RE WORKING HERE!

WE DIDN'T KILL ANYONE!

THAT'S MY BROTHER, WHO JUST FAINTED...

YEAH, THAT'S RIGHT.

SO DO YOU KNOW OF ANY SAFE PLACE WHERE WE COULD SLEEP OR EAT SOMETHING?

YOU CAME ACROSS THE RIGHT PERSON!

I'VE LIVED HERE MY ENTIRE LIFE, SINCE I WAS A LITTLE BOY!

THIS PLACE USED TO BE A FIELD BACK THEN!

...

EHM... IT'S STILL A FIELD.

I KNOW! AND IT'S ALL BECAUSE OF THIS STUPID WAR BETWEEN WITCHES AND ANTI-WITCHCRAFT PEOPLE!
WITHOUT THEIR NONSENSE, WE WOULD BE SUCH A PROSPEROUS COUNTRY!
AND THESE FIELDS WOULD BE FULL OF SCHOOLS, HOSPITALS, LIBRARIES AND MANY, MANY PUBS!
IF ONLY THEY'D LET ME LEARN MAGIC, I'D PUT EVERYONE RIGHT BACK INTO LINE!
YOU! STOP CHATTERING AND GET BACK TO WORK!
SLAP
THE BRIDGE WON'T BUILD ITSELF!!
AND YOU, GUYS, IF YOU'RE LOOKING FOR A PLACE TO STAY, JUST GO SOUTH.
YOU'LL BE AT THE VILLAGE IN THREE HOURS.
THANKS A LOT, SIR!
GOOD LUCK!
EH... DID YOU NOTICE?
THOSE DUDES... THOSE DUDES WEREN'T WITCHES, OF COURSE. BUT THEY DIDN'T SEEM AFRAID OF MAGIC.
AH, THAT'S TRUE!
YES, I'VE ALSO NOTICED THAT! HOW COOL!
YEAH, IT'S...
IT'S WEIRD.
BESIDES, THIS VILLAGE WAS PROBABLY TAKEN BY DANI'S ARMY...
MANY PEOPLE LIVE ON THE STREET,
HALF OF THE BUILDINGS WERE BURNT DOWN.
THEY'VE BEEN THROUGH QUITE A LOT, AND THEY SEEM AFRAID OF THE QUEEN AND HER PEOPLE. YET...
...

EH, THEY SAID THERE ARE VACANT ROOMS!

AWESOME! WE'RE LUCKY!

TOMORROW WE'LL HAVE TO DEAL WITH A COMPLICATED MISSION.

AND WHAT IS THAT...?

TELLING DORIAN WHAT HAPPENED.

MAKING HIM UNDERSTAND THAT HE'S BEEN ASLEEP FOR THREE YEARS.

DO YOU THINK HE'LL TAKE IT WELL? OR WILL HE GO CRAZY?

YES, HE'LL MANAGE.

I'M SURE HE'LL HELP US ALL WITH DANI.

SO... ARE YOU HUNGRY?

DO YOU WANNA GO DOWN AND EAT SOMETHING?

YEAH, I'M STARVING.

WHAT ARE WE GONNA DO WITH THIS ONE, THEN?

YEAH... WE CAN'T GO DOWN WITH THE MASTER TIED UP LIKE A CRIMINAL...

WE'RE WALKING AROUND WITH AN OLD MAN TIED UP AND SOME KIND OF PASSED-OUT ZOMBIE ON OUR BACKS. I'M ACTUALLY SURPRISED THEY DIDN'T

BUT WE CAN'T RISK UNTYING HIM. WE NEED TO KEEP AN EYE ON HIM FOR NOW.
TOMORROW MORNING WE'LL HEAD TO MONICA'S CASTLE, AND WE'LL LOCK HIM UP IN THE DUNGEON.
HEY, DON'T TALK AS IF I'M NOT EVEN HERE...
SINCE WE WILL BE TAKING PENDRAGON TO THE DUNGEON, IT LOOKS LIKE WE WILL ACTUALLY BE ABLE TO ATTEND WILLIAM AND MONICA'S WEDDING.
OH, THAT'S COOL!
MY BROTHER AND MOTHER WILL DEFINITELY BE THERE!
HERE'S WHAT YOU'VE ASKED FOR.
THANKS!
OH, AND JUST A QUESTION...
ARE YOU WITCHES, BY ANY CHANCE?

HUUUUUH? WHAT SHOULD WE SAY??
IF WE SAY YES, WILL THEY KILL US?
I KNEW IT.
OH NO.
IF WE SAY NO, WILL THEY KILL US?
AH... THANK YOU! WE'LL BRING THE DINNER UPSTAIRS!
DON'T MIND HER, SHE DOESN'T KNOW WHAT SHE'S TALKING ABOUT!
YES, WE ARE EXHAUSTED!
BUT DAD...!
LET'S GO.
SOMETHING IS WEIRD HERE.
VERY WEIRD.
ARGH! STUPID BLINDS!!
WHO LEFT THE BLINDS OPEN?!
UH...
WHAT TIME IS IT...?
DORIAN...
...
DORIAN?!
NICO, WHAT'S GOING ON?!

DORIAN DISAPPEARED!! HE'S NOT HERE!!

ARE YOU KIDDING ME?!

OH, HE WAS KIDNAPPED!

WHERE IS THAT IDIOT?!

MMH?

OH...?

AH, GUYS, YOU FINALLY WOKE UP!

I CAN'T BELIEVE IT!

WHAT...?

WHAT HAPPENED TO MY FACE?!

AND MY HAIR?!

AGH, I LOOK DREADFUL! AND... I LOOK WEIRD... MAYBE... TALLER...?

STEP

STEP

STEP

WHAT'S GOING ON...?

THIS CAN'T BE...

WHAT'S ALL THAT NOISE...?
IS SOMEONE TRYING TO STEAL?!
KRACK
CRASH
HEY! WHO'S THERE?
HURRY UP, I NEED TO READ A NEWSPAPER!!
AAAARGH!! A GHOST, IT'S A GHOST!!
NO, I JUST...
NO, IT'S THE DYING BOY OUR LAST GUESTS WERE CARRYING AROUND!
GROOOOOOOOOOOOWWWWL!
HUH? ARE YOU HUNGRY?
DO YOU WANT SOME SOUP?
Y-YES, PLEASE. THANK YOU, MISS.

WELL, YOU WERE REALLY STARVING.
YOU'RE LOOKING BETTER NOW!
I NEED TO GO. THANK YOU FOR EVERYTHING!
EH, YOU'VE GOT TO PAY FOR THE FOOD, KID!
I DON'T HAVE ANY MONEY ON ME.
BUT MY FRIENDS ARE SLEEPING UPSTAIRS! THEY'LL PAY.
WILL YOU COME BACK...?
YES.
BUT BEFORE THAT, THERE'S SOMETHING IMPORTANT I NEED TO DO...
PAQUITA HAIRDRESSER
ARE YOU SURE YOU WANNA CUT IT?
I'M SURE, CUT IT.
DON'T DO IT. IT'S SUCH A SHAME!
LONG HAIR SUITS YOU WELL...
I CAN'T GO OUT LIKE THIS; I LOOK LIKE A CRIMINAL.
MY FATHER WOULD FREAK OUT...
ALL RIGHT THEN...

EVEN THOUGH SOMETHING IS STILL OFF...

PERFECT, I LOOK SO MUCH BETTER!

NOW I CAN RECOGNIZE MYSELF!

EH... EXCUSE ME... HOW OLD DO I LOOK?

WELL, I DON'T KNOW... SIXTEEN? SEVENTEEN?

SIXTEEN?!

THAT MEANS I SLEPT FOR THREE YEARS??

IS SHE ALIVE...?

AGH... I NEED TO KNOW...

BUT I CAN'T JUST ASK... I DON'T KNOW ABOUT THE CURRENT SITUATION.

I DON'T EVEN KNOW WHAT YEAR IT IS OR WHERE I AM. IT COULD BE DANGEROUS.

I'LL JUST GO WAKE UP NICO AND THE OTHERS... OR...

I HAVE AN IDEA.

DO YOU HAVE A NEWSPAPER BY ANY CHANCE?

WHAT?

A NEWSPAPER?

...

... NO.

THERE'S NO SUCH THING HERE, I DON'T KNOW WHERE YOU GOT THAT INFORMATION.

PLEASE LEAVE.

WHA...?

IT'S FIVE FOR THE HAIRCUT.

AH... I DON'T HAVE ANY MONEY ON ME...

WHAT?!

DID YOU THINK WE'D WORK FOR FREE BECAUSE OF YOUR PRETTY FACE?!

PAY US!!

UHM...

I CAN FIX YOUR WINDOW, IF YOU WANT.

BUT YOU'LL NEED TO LEAVE ME ALONE FOR A SECOND.

I PROMISE I WON'T RUN AWAY. BUT PLEASE, DON'T COME BACK UNTIL I TELL YOU TO DO SO.

... SERIOUSLY, THIS GUY...?

I LOCKED THE DOOR. LET HIM TRY ANYTHING HE WANTS.

OOOOH...

INCREDIBLE...

WELL, I HOPE THIS WORKS AS A PAYMENT!

THANK YOU SO MUCH FOR EVERYTHING!

HE'S A WITCH.

DOES HE THINK WE'RE STUPID??

...

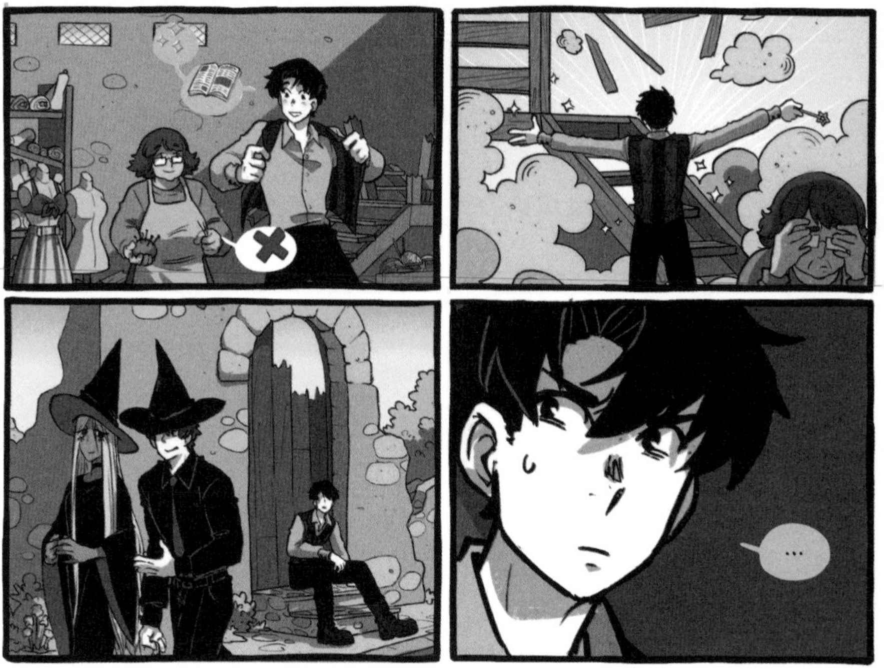

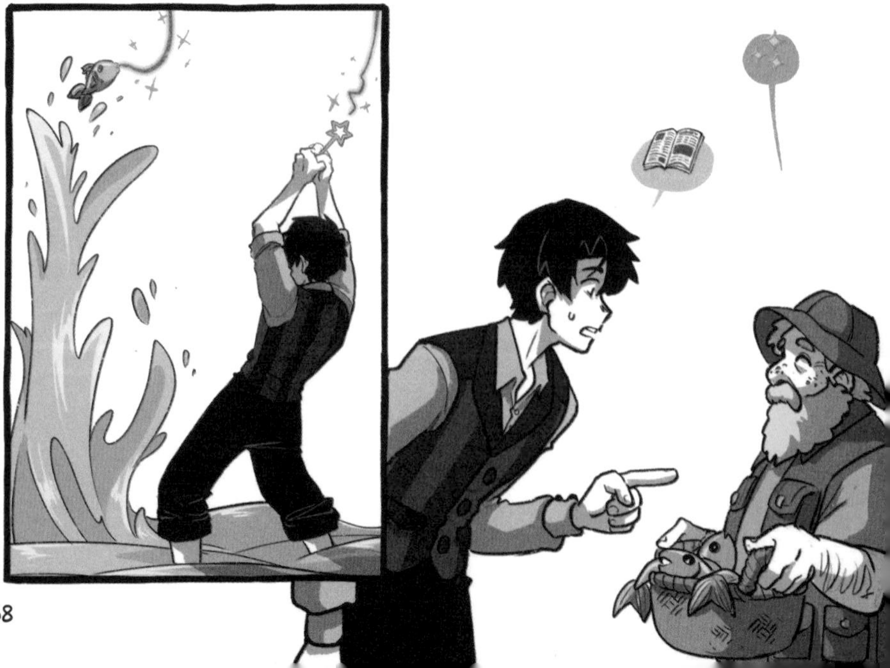

FOLLOW ME, BOY...

AH!

REALLY?

HERE HE IS...

THE YOUNG MAN WHO HAS BEEN CAUSING TROUBLE IN THE VILLAGE ALL MORNING...

EH?

SO YOU'RE LOOKING FOR A NEWSPAPER, MMMH?

LONG TIME NO SEE, DORIAN...

AH?! IT'S YOU!

CHAPTER 63

WHO WAS IT?! WHO WAS HIDING IN THE SWAMP?!

TELL US ALREADY, DORIAN!

YOU DON'T NEED TO RECOUNT YOUR MORNING IN FULL DETAIL!

EH? IT'S QUITE IMPORTANT.

IN THE END, IT TURNED OUT EVERYONE WAS TRYING TO HELP ME, EVEN IF I COULDN'T SEE THAT.

LOOK, I FOUND THE NEWSPAPER.

HMMM...? THIS NEWSPAPER IS...?

ARE THERE ANY ARTICLES ABOUT WITCHCRAFT?

"WEEKLY RECIPE: THIS POTION WILL MAKE YOUR POTATOES GROW IN JUST A FEW HOURS."

WHAT IS THIS...?

THE INSURGENT WITCH

AH! TAKE A LOOK AT THE COVER, MARK...!!

WHAT'S THIS DRAWING RIGHT HERE...?

IT'S ALEX!!

WHAT'S THIS ALL ABOUT?!

... OH!

HI MARK! NICO! LONG TIME NO SEE.

YOU BOTH GREW UP SO FAST!

HEY!

NOAH! BARRY! WHAT ARE YOU DOING HERE?!

DO YOU LIKE OUR SECRET NEWSPAPER?

GENT WITCH

IT'S AN ILLEGAL PUBLICATION.

BUT... WHAT IS IT?

WE THINK THAT THE WITCH'S REIGN IS ONLY ADDING MORE TROUBLE TO THE CONFLICT.

AND WE WANTED TO OFFER A DIFFERENT PERSPECTIVE,

TO SHOW THAT WITCHES DON'T AGREE WITH THE WYTTES' POLICIES.

WELL... MOST OF THE WYTTES.

SORRY, DORIAN.

IT'S OK.

WE PUBLISHED IT FOR THE PEOPLE. ALL OF THE PEOPLE.

WE'RE TRYING TO KEEP IT A SECRET SINCE WE'D END UP AT THE STAKE IF DANI'S ARMY CATCHES US.

THAT'S WHY WE KEEP *THE INSURGENT WITCH* HIDDEN FROM THE OUTSIDERS.
AT LEAST UNTIL WE KNOW THAT WE CAN TRUST THEM.
ALTHOUGH THE ENTIRE VILLAGE KNOWS.
AND WE KNEW RIGHT AWAY THAT WE COULD TRUST THIS YOUNG MAN!
INDEED, HE FIXED MORE HOMES AND BUSINESSES IN ONE DAY THAN WE DID IN A FULL YEAR!
IT'S TRULY AMAZING TO SEE HOW POWERFUL HE IS!
THAT'S TRUE. DORIAN IS A VERY COOL WITCH!
TH... THANK YOU SO MUCH!
NO, MAN. THANK YOU!
SO, DORIAN...
DO YOU ALREADY KNOW EVERYTHING?
ARE YOU AWARE...?
AWARE OF WHAT HAPPENED TO DANI?
... YES.
THERE YOU GO!
THANKS FOR FIXING MY DOGHOUSE!
THANK YOU. IT'S PERFECT.
...

I KNOW I WAS ASLEEP FOR THREE YEARS, FOR SOME REASON.

AND I KNOW THAT DURING THIS TIME, DANI HAS BECOME EVIL.

THEY SAID SHE'S A COLD, CRUEL QUEEN AND THAT SHE DID HORRIBLE THINGS, SHE KILLED PEOPLE.

BUT I DON'T BELIEVE IT.

IT ALL HAS TO DO WITH MY MOTHER.

AND I WILL GO RESCUE HER TODAY.

DORIAN...!

YOU'RE RIGHT, DORIAN. DANI ISN'T EVIL.

BUT SHE IS COLD.

IT'S ALMOST AS IF...

AS IF SHE WERE NOT HERSELF ANYMORE...

SHE HAS BEEN ABSENT SINCE THE MOMENT SHE THOUGHT YOU WERE DEAD.

SO IT'S MY FAULT...

I FAILED HER.

THREE YEARS... I CAN'T BELIEVE IT.

I PROMISED I WOULD GET HER OUT OF THERE AND IT TOOK ME THREE YEARS...

IT'S NOT YOUR FAULT, DORIAN!

NO! IT'S...

IT'S THE MASTER'S FAULT.

BUT NOW THAT YOU'RE HERE, EVERYTHING WILL BE FINE!

I KNOW YOU'RE THE ONLY ONE WHO CAN MAKE DANI COME BACK TO HER SENSES!

SHE'LL GO BACK TO NORMAL AS SOON AS SHE SEES YOU!

YES... I THINK SO TOO.

ALL IS NOT LOST, IT SEEMS...

NOT EVERYONE HATES WITCHES...

ACTUALLY, IT'S PRETTY WEIRD BUT PEOPLE SEEM TO BE A LOT LESS FRIGHTENED NOW!

THAT'S BECAUSE PEOPLE ONLY WANT TO LIVE IN PEACE.

THAT'S SOMETHING WE HAVE IN COMMON.

AND MAGIC IS REALLY CONVENIENT!
MY POTATOES GREW IN JUST 3 HOURS!
AND NOW A HERO HAS ARRIVED!
A HERO?! NO, I AM NOT...!
WE'VE ALSO GOT MONICA'S PLAN.
I'M SURE ONE OF THEM WILL BRING DANI BACK.
IF DORIAN'S THE "HERO", MONICA'S GONNA GET MAD.
SHE ALWAYS SAID SHE WANTED A STATUE BUILT IN HER HONOR IN THE TOWN SQUARE.
AH! SPEAKING OF MONICA...
DORIAN, DO YOU KNOW...?
WELL...!
UM... DO YOU KNOW ANYTHING ABOUT MONICA OR NOT?
HAVE YOU FULLY READ THE NEWSPAPER...?
EH? NOT YET, I WAS DOING THAT WHEN YOU CAME DOWNSTAIRS.
WHY ARE YOU ASKING?
ROYAL WEDDIN
HUH?! WE... WELL... I KNOW SHE'S SAFE AND SOUND IN THE CASTLE OF WILLIAM'S FATHER!
IS THAT RIGHT?

UM... YES...
TRUTH IS, I'VE GIVEN THIS MATTER A LOT OF THOUGHT...
AND I'VE GOT A SERIOUS PROBLEM....
WHAT PROBLEM?
HOW OLD IS MONICA NOW?
EIGHTEEN, JUST LIKE ME.
SHE'S AN ADULT!
HOW AM I SUPPOSED TO TALK TO HER NOW?!
DON'T WORRY, SHE'S DYING TO SEE YOU.
PRECISELY!
I'VE MADE HER WAIT THREE YEARS. IT'S ONLY BEEN A WHILE FOR ME.
I BET SHE'S FURIOUS!

I REMEMBER IT PERFECTLY. IT ONLY HAPPENED A FEW HOURS AGO...

SHE PROMISED SHE'D WAIT FOR ME...

IT LOOKED LIKE...

IT LOOKED LIKE WE WERE BOTH ON THE SAME PAGE...

BUT NOW...

WHAT IS SHE GONNA THINK WHEN SHE SEES ME?!

WHO'S THIS KID?!

DO YOU THINK I'M GONNA PLAY HIDE AND SEEK WITH YOU, DORIAN?

WHAT A FREAK...

SHE'LL THINK I'M RIDICULOUS!

I REALLY DON'T GET ALL THE FUSS... WHAT DIFFERENCE DOES IT MAKE IF IT TOOK YOU A WHILE TO COME BACK?

WAIT, AISHA... IT'S JUST THAT DORIAN AND MONICA...

BESIDES, I'M SURE SHE HAS MORE IMPORTANT THINGS TO THINK ABOUT WITH THE WHOLE WEDDING THING.

HUH?

CHAPTER 64

OH, MONICA, THOSE EARRINGS WILL LOOK WONDERFUL WITH YOUR WEDDING DRESS!

COME ON, ANNE! THEY LOOK TERRIBLE!

THESE ONES SUIT HER BETTER. THEY'RE MORE DELICATE AND ELEGANT.

LET MONICA DECIDE!

COME ON! WHICH ONE'S THE BEST?

THE ONES I CHOSE FOR YOU, RIGHT?

...

MONICA, ANSWER!

I'M SORRY, GIRLS. I HAVE TO GO!!

HUH? WHERE ARE YOU GOING?!

YOU CAN'T GO OUT LIKE THIS! YOU'RE NAKED!

MMMH??

AH! DAMIEN?!

DAMIEN!!

ARE YOU ALREADY BACK?!

HI, MONICA.

AH...

THAT SMILE...

MONICA... LISTEN.

HOW DID IT GO?

WHERE ARE THE OTHERS?

WE FOUND DORIAN.

HE'S ALIVE AND WELL.

VERY STRONG AND DETERMINED TO SAVE DANI.

DORIAN...!

UH...

GOOD MORNING, WILL!
AH! DAMIEN, YOU'RE BACK!
YES.
I KNEW YOU'D BE ON TIME FOR MY WEDDING.
YOU COULDN'T MISS IT!
WELL...
I ACTUALLY CAME HERE TO PUT PENDRAGON IN JAIL,
PREVENT HIM FROM KILLING MORE INNOCENT KIDS.
WH... WHAT?
IT'S A LONG STORY.
AND YOU'RE GETTING MARRIED IN A COUPLE OF HOURS, SO THERE'S NO TIME.

HERE, I'LL HELP YOU WITH THAT.

YOU SEEM QUITE LONELY.

AND YOU SEEM VERY HAPPY.

... OF COURSE.

WE FOUND DORIAN, SAFE AND SOUND.

AT THIS VERY MOMENT HE'S GOING TO RESCUE DANI. LOOKS PROMISING.

...IS THE WEDDING STILL THAT URGENT, THEN?

YES.

IF DORIAN DOESN'T SUCCEED, WE'VE GOT MONICA'S PLAN.

WE CAN'T SUDDENLY CALL OFF THE WEDDING, SPOILING THE WHOLE PLAN.

MOREOVER, SOONER OR LATER, YOU WOULD'VE ENDED UP MARRYING MONICA ANYWAYS, YOU'VE ALWAYS KNOWN THAT.

DOES IT BOTHER YOU?

MY WEDDING, I MEAN.

WHY WOULD IT BOTHER ME?

YOU SAID IT YOURSELF, NOTHING WILL CHANGE. WE'LL STILL BE FRIENDS AS USUAL.

BUT DAMIEN,

WHAT IS IT THAT YOU WANT?

JUST BEING FRIENDS?
WHA...?!
WHAT'S YOUR PROBLEM, WILL?!
WE BOTH KNOW EXACTLY WHAT I WANT!
EH...?
YOU KNOW I LOVE YOU.
SO MUCH.
WHAT WE DON'T KNOW IS WHAT YOU WANT.
I'VE KNOWN FOR YEARS, BUT I STILL ASK MYSELF WHAT'S ON YOUR MIND.

WHAT DO YOU WANT, WILL?

THAT DOESN'T ANSWER MY QUESTION.

BONG BON

WHAT DO I WANT...?

BONG BONG

I NEED TO MARRY PRINCESS MONICA.

IT'S IMPORTANT TO THE KINGDOM.

BONG

DORIAN...
IS IT A MISTAKE TO MARRY WILLIAM?
I PROMISED I'D WAIT FOR YOU, BUT...
THE FUTURE OF OUR KINGDOM...
DEPENDS ON THIS...
AND AFTER ALL, YOU KNOW I'M GONNA GET MARRIED, DON'T YOU?

YET YOU'VE CHOSEN TO RESCUE DANI INSTEAD OF TRYING TO STOP THE WEDDING.

IT MAKES SENSE.

WHAT HAPPENED BETWEEN US TOOK PLACE A LONG TIME AGO...

IT WAS JUST CHILD'S PLAY...

AND NOW...

I HAVE EVERYTHING PLANNED DOWN TO THE LAST DETAIL.

THE PERFECT DRESS.

THE IDEAL BANQUET.

I'M ABOUT TO BECOME A MARRIED WOMAN.

THE PEOPLE ARE EUPHORIC.

ALMOST ALL MY LOVED ONES ARE HERE.
MY PERFECT WEDDING, AND YET...
YOU MAY KISS THE BRIDE.
IT'S DONE.
HUSBAND AND WIFE.
NOT SO FAST.

WE DON'T NEED ANY OTHER QUEENS IN THESE LANDS, PRINCESS MONICA.
AH! WHO ARE THOSE LADIES?
THEY'VE STOPPED THE ROYAL WEDDING!
THEY'RE WITCHES!
AH!
DANI...!
WELL, I AM AFRAID YOU GOT HERE A BIT TOO LATE!
MMH...?
NOT AT ALL...

WE GOT HERE AT THE RIGHT TIME.
COME ON, EVERYONE, MOVE TOWARDS QUEEN MONICA!
KILL THE QUEEN AND THE KING!
KILL AS MANY PEOPLE AS YOU CAN!
OF COURSE... THE WYTTES' ARMY.
IS THAT DANI?
I CAN'T RECOGNIZE HER...
NICO WAS RIGHT.
DANI...
SHE LOOKS ABSENT.
AGGHH!! HURRY UP, TAKE COVER!
OVER HERE, QUICK!!
NICO WAS RIGHT ABOUT EVERYTHING...

HOW CAN YOU ALLOW THIS, DANI?
ARE YOU THERE?
WHAT HAVE THEY DONE TO YOU?
I HOPE MY PLAN WORKS...
RUN, GET OVER THERE!
REMEMBER THE REHEARSALS!
THEY'LL SEE!
YOU SAID IT'D BE A WONDERFUL WEDDING!
IF ONLY I HAD KNOWN, I'D HAVE SIGNED UP FOR YOUR MOTHER'S PICNIC!
IS EVERYONE READY?
YES! NOW, MR. DAMIEN!

LOOK! THERE'S THE QUEEN MOTHER!

TAKE HER, I HATE HER BORED EXPRESSION!

THEY'VE LOCKED US UP!!

UH? MAGIC?

WAIT, THERE'S SOMETHING WEIRD...

HOW?!

THIS CAN'T BE...

THIS SPELL...!

DAMIEN!

THE RIGHT MOMENT, YOU SAID?

INDEED.

YOU GOT HERE JUST IN TIME FOR THE PARTY.

I'VE ALSO GOT A POINTY HAT, YOU KNOW?
HEH...
LUCKILY, I HAD IT ALL READY.
NOW!
NO!
TOWARDS QUEEN DANI!

HE HIT THE QUEEN!

...

DO YOU THINK IT WORKED?

WHAT'S THAT? A LIQUID?!

IT'S A POTION!

AH!

NO!

NOT A SINGLE DROP TOUCHED HER!

HA-HA!
IS THAT A BARRIER...?
WHAT KIND OF SPELL IS THAT?
WHERE DID SHE LEARN HOW TO DO THAT?
LET ME DEAL WITH THIS!
YOU CAN HELP EVACUATE THE CASTLE AND ITS SURROUNDINGS, MONICA.
NO!
DON'T EVEN THINK OF ATTACKING DANI WITH THAT!
I DON'T WANNA KILL HER! JUST OVERCOME HER.
I HAVEN'T SPENT YEARS STUDYING POTIONS ONLY TO SEE THAT HER SKIN WASN'T TOUCHED BY A SINGLE DROP!
I NEED TO TRY.

DON'T WORRY, WILL!
DAMIEN HAS EVERYTHING UNDER CONTROL.
WITCHES CAN'T GET OUT OF THE PROTECTIVE SHIELD...
AH!
MONICA!!
NO!
DID SHE HIT HER?
OH NO!

PRINCESS MONICA!

QUEEN MONICA'S HURT!

QUICK, I HAVE TO DO SOMETHING!

GOOD JOB, MR. DAMIEN!

HE HAS CAUGHT THE WITCH!

YOU'RE TRAPPED!

NOW WHAT, HUH, WITCH QUEEN?

HA-HA...

... HA.

OH.

IT'S OK TO LEND ME YOUR POWERS, BUT...

COULD YOU DO SOMETHING ON YOUR OWN FOR ONCE?

97

KILL HER NOW, DANI!
HURRY UP AND KILL QUEEN MONICA!
UGH...
NO...
PLEASE, REMEMBER...
IT'S ME, MONICA!
THIS CAN'T BE...
IS SHE REALLY LIKE THIS BECAUSE SHE THOUGHT DORIAN HAD DIED?
DIE.
UH... THAT DIDN'T WORK...
WELL, I'VE GOT A BETTER IDEA...

SINCE YOU'RE SO CLOSE NOW...
UGH!
DRINK THIS!
?!
CHEERS!
HOPE IT DOESN'T TASTE TOO BAD!
NO!
HAVE YOU POISONED MY DAUGHTER?!
YOU'LL PAY FOR THIS!!
DID SHE SUCCEED...?
GREAT, THAT'S MY QUEEN!
I KNEW YOU WOULDN'T DISAPPOINT ME!
GREAT!

AH... DID IT WORK...?
UH...
UGH...
YUCK...
UH...
DANI...?
A... ARE YOU OK?
DANI...
DON'T TOUCH ME.
DANI?!
LET GO, YOU'RE HURTING ME!
I'M SORRY IF IT TASTED BAD, DON'T PUKE IT UP THOUGH!

DANI, ARE YOU OK...?
DANI...?
DANI WHO?
EH?!
OH, LOOK, THE LITTLE PRINCESS...
I REMEMBER YOU VERY WELL, KID...

I'VE SEEN YOUR GREATEST FEARS...
WH...?
WHAT?
WHO ARE YOU?
YOU'RE NOT DANI...
YES, YOUR FEARS...
CAN'T YOU REMEMBER ME?
YOUR FEARS ARE SO CHILDISH,
SO SELFISH
AND STUPID.
THAT'S...
YOU'RE PATHETIC.
THAT'S NOT TRUE!!
I'M NOT LIKE THAT ANYMORE!

GET OUT OF HERE, STUPID KID.
YOU CAN'T DEAL WITH THIS.
LET'S GO.

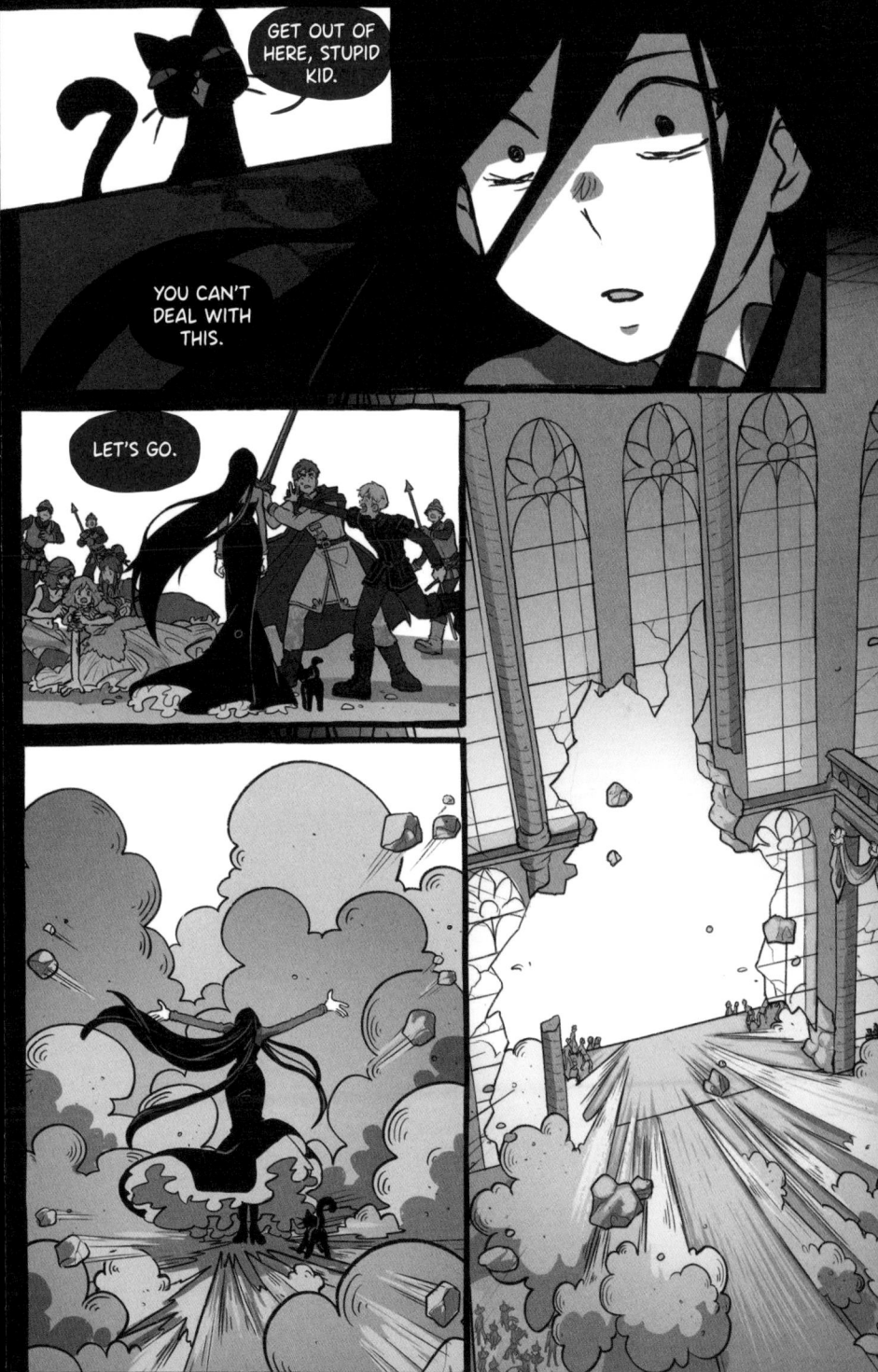

WE'LL NEED TO MOVE ON TO PLAN B AND USE OUR JOINED ARMIES.

WE'LL HAVE WAY MORE SUPPORT NOW THAT WE'RE MARRIED.

AH... SHE GOT AWAY.

SHE DESTROYED THE CATHEDRAL... MONICA'S PLAN DIDN'T WORK, IN THE END...

...

THAT'S NOT TRUE...

MY PLAN ACTUALLY DID SOMETHING.

ISN'T THAT TRUE, MRS. WYTTE...?

CHAPTER 65

WE'RE ALMOST THERE! I CAN'T BELIEVE IT; I'LL FINALLY SEE DANI!

WOW... I REMEMBERED THIS PALACE WAY... BRIGHTER.

HAVE YOU BEEN HERE BEFORE?

OF COURSE! I'VE SPENT MANY SUMMERS HERE.

MY BROTHER AND I WOULD SPEND THE DAY PLAYING WITH MONICA, WILL, DAMIEN, IVY AND ANNE.

OH, I WAS ONLY HERE ONCE.

THE DAY OF THE GREAT BALL THE KING ORGANIZED IN HOPES OF REESTABLISHING PEACE DURING THE WAR AGAINST WITCHES...

IT DIDN'T GO WELL.

CLEARLY.

WHAT MATTERS THE MOST IS HOW MARK WAS DRESSED THAT DAY!

I'LL REMEMBER THOSE SILLY LITTLE PINK PANTS 'TIL THE DAY I DIE!

HA-HA!

I NEED TO SEE THAT.
NO! TRUST ME, YOU DON'T WANNA SEE THAT.
HE WAS ALSO WEARING A GIANT RIBBON AROUND HIS NECK!
AND FLOWERS ON HIS LAPEL!
STOP MAKING FUN OF ME!!
AH! THAT'S TRUE. YOU LOOKED VERY ELEGANT, JUST LIKE A PRINCE!
...
YOU TOO, DORIAN?!
AISHA, STOP LOOKING AT ME LIKE THAT!
HERE WE ARE.
THIS IS WHERE DANI USUALLY SITS IN FRONT OF THE WINDOW.
WHAT A GLOOMY PLACE.
KEEP YOUR EYES OPEN.
IT'S STRANGE THAT WE HAVEN'T RUN INTO ANYONE YET.
AH! THERE SHE IS!
DANI...?
IT'S ME, DORIAN.
I'M SORRY IT...
IT TOOK ME SO LONG...

OOOOH! OF COURSE I KNOW WHO YOU ARE, YOUNG MAN!
I'M GLAD YOU'VE FINALLY DECIDED TO JOIN YOUR FAMILY!
WHA...?!
UH...
UGH...
WAAAAH! DANIII!
WHAT HAVE I DONE TO YOU?!
YOU LOOK SO OLD AND TIRED, IT'S MY FAULT!
ALL THOSE YEARS ALONG WITH THE SADNESS OF MY LOSS LEFT SUCH A BIG MARK ON YOU!
I'M SO SORRY, DANI! PLEASE, FORGIVE ME!
WHAT ARE YOU TALKING ABOUT, DORIAN?! THAT'S AN OLD WOMAN!!
THAT'S NOT DANI!
HUH? REALLY?
I'M AFRAID NOT, YOUNG MAN! YOUR SISTER'S IN ANOTHER CASTLE!

BUT...

WHERE?

...

WILL...

CAN YOU JUST STOP STARING AT ME?

YOU'RE GETTING ON MY NERVES. IF YOU DON'T STOP, I'LL KICK YOUR ASS.

THIS IS NOT ACCEPTABLE!

MONICA!!

...

YOU CAN'T KILL MRS. WYTTE!

SHE'S DAMIEN'S MUM! AND DORIAN'S AND DANIELA'S! IF YOU LOVE THEM, YOU CAN'T DO THIS!

WELL, IT'S NOT JUST MY CHOICE TO MAKE.

REMEMBER YOU ARE THE KING NOW.

WELL, THEN... I FORBID YOU!

WILLIAM... DROP IT.

THAT'S NOT HOW YOU FIX THINGS.

LOOK.

DON'T ASSUME I'VE SPENT YEARS STUDYING, RESEARCHING, AND IMPROVING...

... JUST TO MAKE A SLIGHTLY STRONGER HEALING POTION.

NO...

I'VE STILL GOT MANY ACES UP MY SLEEVE.

WHAT ARE YOU GONNA DO WITH THAT?

WHAT'S THAT POTION FOR?

MONICA!

...

TAKE IT.

YES, YOUR MAJESTY.

YOU ALREADY KNOW WHAT TO DO WITH IT.

BE DISCREET.

AT YOUR SERVICE, YOUR MAJESTY.

WE'RE HERE...

LAST TIME I WAS HERE FEELS LIKE YESTERDAY!

ONE SECOND, MARK, I NEED TO PUT THE LITTLE ONE IN MY BACKPACK!

HE COULD SCARE SOMEBODY IF THEY SEE HIM...

YOU SHOULD NAME HIM! GIVE HIM A POWERFUL NAME! LIKE BLOODY OR MONSTROUS...

COME ON, GET IN! BE GOOD. LOOK HOW CARLO'S HIDING!

YES, NICO TOO! I'M SURE THEY'D BE SCARED OF HIS FIERCENESS IF THEY SAW HIM...

THAT'S ENOUGH, IDIOT! I'D LIKE TO SEE YOU WITH MY SIZE!!

DEATH WING...

DEVIL...

TORMENT OF HEAVENS...

BREATH OF HELL...

I WOULDN'T BE AS CUTE AS YOU, THAT'S FOR SURE.

WOW... EVERYTHING'S BASICALLY THE SAME...

EVEN THOUGH IT'S CLEAR THAT DANI'S ARMY HASN'T CONQUERED THESE LANDS YET...

PEOPLE SEEM VERY QUIET.

UH...

IT WAS HERE...

THE PLACE WHERE THEY WERE GONNA KILL ME FOR WITCHCRAFT...

WHERE I SAW MONICA FOR THE LAST TIME...

WHERE DANI THOUGHT I...

IT'S WEIRD TO KNOW SO MUCH TIME HAS PASSED...

YOU'RE GONNA DIE, FOOLISH!

I'LL AVENGE MY SISTERS WHO DIED AT THE STAKE!!

NOOO, HELP!

HUH...

WHAT?!

...

WHAT A GAME...

MUAHAHA! YOU CAN'T RUN AWAY!

GET READY TO SUFFER MY WICKED MAGIC!

STOP, YOU EVIL WITCH!

OOOOH!

YES, IT'S ACTUALLY ME!! QUEEN MONICA, THE GOOD WITCH!! I'VE COME TO RESCUE YOU!!

I'M A GOOD WITCH TOO, LOOK! I'VE GOT A WAND!

THANK YOU, QUEEN MONICA!

YOUR POSH MAGIC CAN'T DEFEAT ME, LITTLE PRINCESS!

I'M NOT A PRINCESS, I'M A QUEEN!

AND YOU FELL INTO MY TRAP!! COME ON, SERVANTS, THROW THE POTION AT HER!

NOOOO!

HA-HA!

DORIAN? WHAT ARE YOU DOING?!

COME ON!

AH, SORRY!

I'M COMING!

ACCORDING TO THE LOCALS, DANI WAS HERE.

YES, AND SHE DESTROYED THE CATHEDRAL!

THAT'S SCARY...

IT SEEMS THAT I ALWAYS ARRIVE TOO LATE.

DON'T FEEL DISCOURAGED, MAN. WE HAD TO TRY IT!

I TOLD YOU DANI WOULD BE AT THE WEDDING!

WHOA! WHAT'S GOING ON?!

WITCHCRAFT!

THEY'RE SPIES OF QUEEN DANI!

WHAT THE...?!

WOOOW!

AHA! NOW YOU CAN FINALLY SEE MY REAL HEIGHT!

YOU'RE GOING TO BITE THE DUST, MARK! SEE WHO'S TALLER NOW!

...

...I DON'T WANT TO HEAR A WORD.

ANYWAY, THIS MUST MEAN THAT DANI IS HERE SOMEWHERE.

I ALWAYS GO BACK TO MY NORMAL SIZE WHEN SHE'S AROUND.

!

NO...

THIS CAN'T BE...

IS HE...?

UH...

WAA...!

...

MONICA!

IT'S DORIAN!

UGH.

IT'S DORIAN!

HE'S BACK!

IT'S HIM...

IT'S...

HIM?

WAAA...

SHE'S...

SHE'S SO...

TINY.

WAAAA!

HEY, YOU...!

IS IT REALLY YOU?

EH?

IT'S ME, DORIAN.

HUH, YES...

HIS VOICE.

IT SOUNDS SO DEEP!

BUT YES, IT'S REALLY HIM.

I'M SO SORRY...ABOUT DISAPPEARING FOR SO LONG.

I... MMMH...

THERE'S NO DOUBT.

THIS IS SO WEIRD...

I'VE DREAMT OF THIS MOMENT FOR SO LONG.

I JUST WANT TO HUG HIM AGAIN,

I WANNA CHECK IF HE'S TRULY ALIVE.

BUT...

WOULD THAT BE OK? HUGGING THIS PERSON?

HE LOOKS SO DIFFERENT. I FEEL WEIRD.

UH... MONICA...

THIS...

THIS IS NOT WHAT I WAS EXPECTING...

I WONDER WHAT IT FEELS LIKE TO HUG HIM.

ARE YOU ANGRY?

EH? NO, OF COURSE N...!

MONICA, LOOK!! THE SPELL SUDDENLY BROKE!!

NICO!! YOU'RE SO HANDSOME AND SUPER TALL!

I AM, AM I NOT?

OH, I'M SO GLAD!

HOW DID YOU GO BACK TO NORMAL?!

THAT'S WHY WE WERE WONDERING IF YOU HAD CAPTURED DANI OR...

I DON'T REALLY KNOW. I DIDN'T DO ANYTHING!

IF YOU HAD HEALED HER OR SOMETHING.

HI, MONICA!

ACTUALLY NO. DANI RAN AWAY BEFORE I COULD DO ANYTHING...

I DON'T KNOW WHERE SHE IS...

AW, HELLO SWEET CARLO! LONG TIME NO SEE!

...

I KNEW IT.

SHE HATES ME.

CHAPTER 66

WHOAAAA!
INCREDIBLE!
WHAT AN AWESOME SECRET LAB, MONICA!
YOU'VE GOT EVERYTHING HERE!!
HU HU, I KNOW.
WHAT ABOUT THESE NOTES? DID YOU WRITE ALL OF THEM?!
I HOPE YOU'RE PROUD OF ME, PROFESSOR WYTTE.
YES, I AM.
I'M TRULY AMAZED.
THIS IS BRILLIANT, MONICA.
OH NO OH NO OH NO OH NO
HE ACTUALLY LOOKS LIKE A TEACHER NOW!

YOU KNOW... ALL THIS...
I DID IT IN ORDER TO SAVE DANI.
I PROMISED YOU I'D STAY OUT OF THIS, BUT IT'S BEEN A LONG TIME...
AT SOME POINT I LOST HOPE AND I THOUGHT YOU WOULDN'T COME BACK,
I COULDN'T JUST SIT AND WAIT.
I'M SO SORRY, MONICA.
UH?
IT HURTS TO HAVE BEEN GONE FOR THREE YEARS...
I STILL CAN'T PROCESS IT.
DON'T SAY SORRY... I DIDN'T MEAN TO...!
IT WASN'T YOUR FAULT! IT WAS THE MASTER'S!
TO ME, IT FEELS LIKE EVERYTHING HAPPENED YESTERDAY, AND YET...
YOU GUYS WENT THROUGH SO MUCH...
EVERYTHING HAS CHANGED QUITE A LOT.
I FEEL SO INCREDIBLY OUT OF PLACE... MORE THAN EVER.
YOU'RE NOT OUT OF PLACE!
WE WERE ALL WAITING FOR YOU!
YOU'RE THE ONLY ONE WHO CAN BRING DANI BACK!
AS SOON AS SHE SEES THAT YOU'RE ALIVE, SHE'LL GO BACK TO NORMAL!

WE NEED TO GET THIS OVER WITH ONCE AND FOR ALL!
UH...
YOU'RE RIGHT.
LET'S SAVE HER.
WHAT A CLICHÉ.
THIS IS MY CHANCE TO GET OUT OF HERE.
BUT WITHOUT MY WAND, THOUGH...

MMH?

OH, COME ON...

CLICK

THEY'RE SO USELESS.

I COULD GET RID OF THEM ONCE AND FOR ALL, IF I WANTED TO.

IT'S TOO MUCH OF A MESS, THOUGH.

I'D BETTER NOT MAKE THINGS MORE COMPLICATED.

UH...

ALL RIGHT...

PERFECT.

BUT FIRST...

I NEED TO FIND DANI!

WHERE COULD SHE BE?

I THINK I'LL PAY A VISIT TO QUEEN MONICA...

TWO BIRDS WITH ONE STONE.
...
HOW EASY...
THE KING AND THE QUEEN MUST BE ASLEEP...
AND HOW IRONIC...
YOU'RE GOING TO DIE THE SAME WAY YOUR FATHER DID, MONICA.
AND YOU'LL NEVER HURT A WITCH AGAIN.

THIS IS NECESSARY, FOR OUR SAKE!
EH?!
SHE'S NOT HERE?!
WERE YOU LOOKING FOR ME, MRS. WYTTE?
WHAT...?!
YES, I WAS LOOKING FOR YOU, MONICA!
STOP, MUM.
DON'T ATTACK THE QUEEN, OR I'LL CURSE YOU.

DAMIEN... YOU...
WHAT'S ALL OF THIS...?
WHY DID YOU COME HERE MUM?
COULDN'T YOU SIMPLY ESCAPE?
AFTER WHAT THESE PEOPLE HAVE DONE TO US, DAMIEN?
NO, THEY MUST PAY...
YOU KNOW PERFECTLY WELL THAT MANY WITCHES DIED AT THE STAKE...
EVEN...
EVEN YOUR BROTHER... HE...
IT WAS HERE WHERE THEY BURNED HIM.
BUT IT WASN'T ME, MRS. WYTTE.
I'D HAVE NEVER HURT DORI--
I DON'T CARE!
THE OLD KING DID IT...

... AND YOU AND YOUR HUSBAND COULD DECIDE TO FOLLOW IN HIS STEPS ANY DAY NOW!
I DON'T KNOW WHAT YOU'RE TRYING TO SHOW WITH THIS AMBUSH...
HEY...!
NO! WAIT!
...BUT YOU SHOULDN'T HAVE LEFT THE WANDS WITHIN MY REACH!
I WON'T ALLOW YOU TO BECOME MONSTERS LIKE YOUR PARENTS!
DIE!

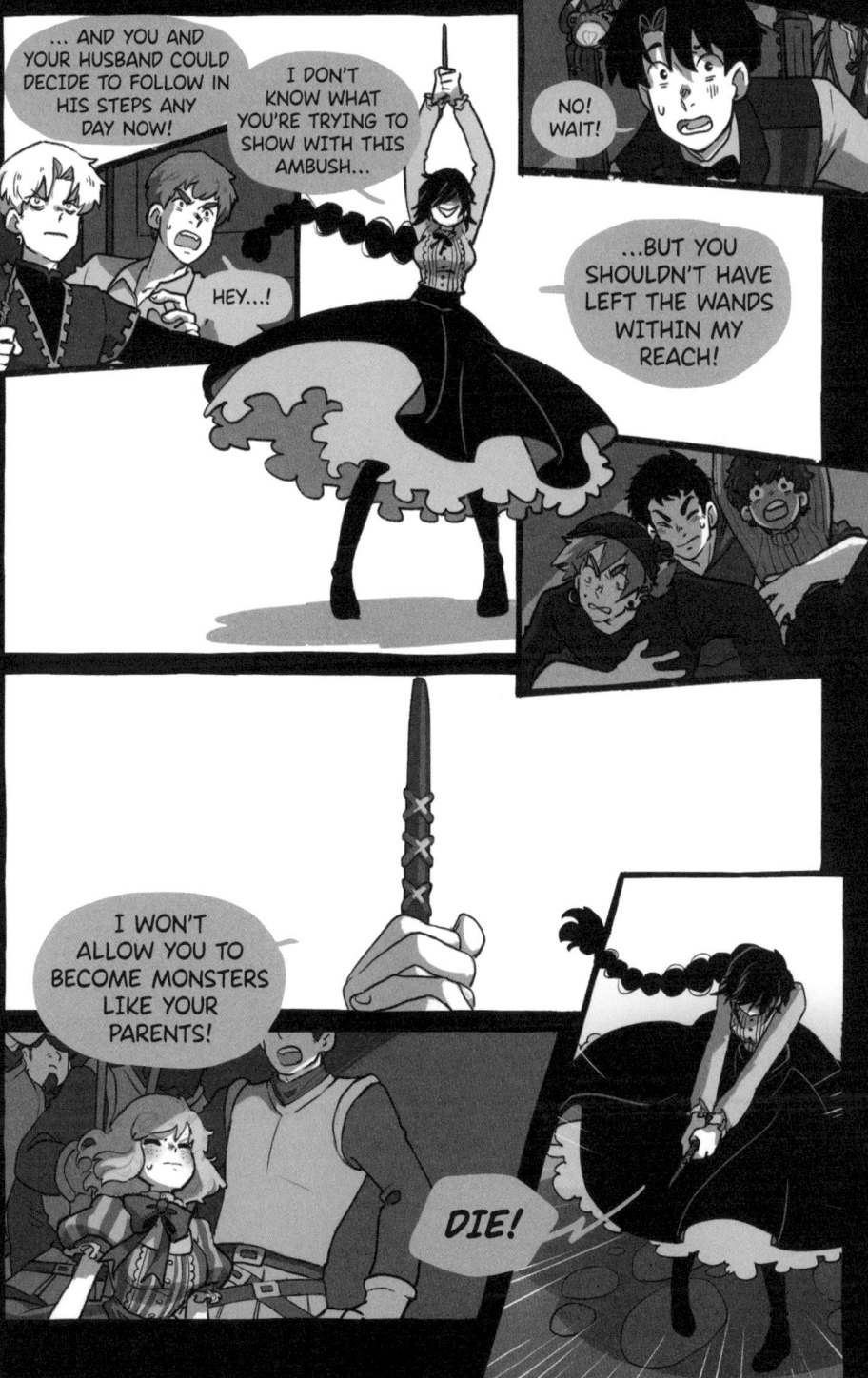

...
WHAT?
WHY IS IT NOT WORKING?
STUPID WAND!
WORK!
KILL HER!
KILL HER!
WORK, DAMMIT!!

IT'S OVER, MRS. WYTTE. SURRENDER.
...
WHAT HAVE YOU DONE TO ME?
I'VE POISONED YOU.
YOU SHOULDN'T HAVE EATEN THE DINNER WE SERVED YOU.
IT CONTAINED A POTION...
...SPECIFICALLY MADE TO SUPPRESS THE POWERS OF THE PERSON WHO INGESTED IT.
FOREVER.
WE NEEDED TO SEE IF YOUR POWERS WERE REALLY GONE.
NO... THIS CAN'T BE...
AS FAR AS I CAN TELL, IT WORKED.
YOU'RE NOT A WITCH ANYMORE.
I'LL KILL YOU!

MUM, THAT'S IT. IT'S OVER.

STOP!

JUST STOP IT.

YOU LOST.

DAMIEN... WHY...?

WHY WERE YOU NEVER ON OUR SIDE...?

WHY DID YOU ABANDON ME?

I CAN'T HELP YOU WITH YOUR VENGEFUL CRUSADE. IT'S TOO MUCH. IT'S JUST GONNA HURT YOU EVEN MORE.

THEY'RE THE ONES WHO HURT ME, DAMIEN.

AND YOUR BROTHER. AND YOUR DAD.

WHAT HAPPENED TO DAD WAS AN ACCIDENT.

AND DORIAN ISN'T...

IT DOESN'T MATTER ANYMORE...

I HAVEN'T GOT ANYTHING LEFT...

MUM...! PLEASE...

DAMIEN...?
UGH...
I JUST WANTED MY MOTHER BACK. I JUST WANTED YOU TO FORGIVE.
I WANTED YOU TO...
FORGIVE ME.
PLEASE... LET ME HELP YOU.

MUM...
ARE YOU...?!
YES, MUM.
IT'S ME, DORIAN.
MY LITTLE BOY, YOU'RE OK!
WHAT HAVE YOU DONE TO DANI, MUM?
NOTHING!
...
OKAY.

I'M SO GLAD WE'RE TOGETHER AGAIN.
MUM... TONIGHT YOU'LL SLEEP IN MY ROOM.
DON'T TRY ANYTHING FUNNY. THE GUARDS WILL ESCORT US.
... FINE.
...
AH! OF COURSE!
NOW I KNOW WHY DANI'S CURSE BROKE TODAY!
DO YOU?
DANI CURSED ME A LONG TIME AGO IN ORDER TO PROTECT ME FROM HER MOTHER!
NOW THAT SHE HAS LOST HER POWERS, I'M NO LONGER IN DANGER!
WHAT DID YOU CALL ME?
HOW UNBELIEVABLY SMART OF YOU, NICO!
WHAT DO YOU MEAN, UNBELIEVABLY?!

WHERE DID MONICA GO?

SHE WAS A BIT WEIRD...

MONICA...?

WHAT'S WRONG?!

ARE YOU ALL RIGHT?!

YOU'RE SO PALE! ARE YOU FEELING DIZZY?

I'M FINE, I'M FINE!

BUT...!

DON'T TOUCH ME!

DORIAN...!

LEAVE ME ALONE, I'M FINE.
YOU'RE NOT FINE! LOOK AT YOURSELF, YOU'RE SHIVERING!
PLEASE...!
... WHAT'S THE MATTER?
ALL WENT WELL, MONICA!
YOU MAY BE RIGHT... EVERYTHING WENT WELL.
ALTHOUGH... DO YOU KNOW HOW MANY PEOPLE TRIED THAT POTION BEFORE YOUR MOTHER, DORIAN?
NOBODY!
IT COULD HAVE BADLY HURT HER!!
AND DID YOU SEE HER FACE?!
HOW CAN I MAKE SURE I DID THE RIGHT THING?!
WHAT IF YOUR MOTHER'S RIGHT?
WHAT IF I BECOME A MONSTER?
I DON'T LIKE THIS.
I'VE ONLY BEEN THE QUEEN FOR A COUPLE OF DAYS, AND MAYBE I'VE ALREADY MADE TERRIBLE DECISIONS.
I CAN'T DO THIS...!

AH...
STOP SAYING THOSE THINGS ABOUT YOURSELF.
LISTEN, I...
I'VE READ YOUR NOTES ABOUT POTIONS. YOU STUDIED AS MUCH AS POSSIBLE.
YOU WOULDN'T HAVE GIVEN HER A POTION WITHOUT TRUSTING YOUR ABILITIES.
AND YOU ALSO PUT YOURSELF IN DANGER.
IF THE POTION HADN'T WORKED, YOU...
...YOU COULD HAVE BEEN KILLED BY MY MOTHER IN THAT ROOM.
BUT YOU STOOD FIRM AND TRUSTED YOURSELF.
...
DORIAN, THAT'S...
... AND I ALSO TRUST YOU, MONICA.
IT IS NOT EASY TO MAKE DECISIONS IN THE MIDST OF A WAR.
BUT I BELIEVE WHAT YOU DID WAS THE BEST SOLUTION.
MY MOTHER LET HER POWERS DEFINE HER ENTIRE IDENTITY.
NOW SHE WILL HAVE TO REBUILD HERSELF.
AND EVEN THOUGH I STILL DON'T TRUST HER, WE ARE A FAMILY.

AS SOON AS I FIND DANI, WE'LL REBUILD EVERYTHING TOGETHER.

PHEW...

OH... ARE YOU FEELING BETTER?

YES... WAY BETTER.

AH, UM... SORRY FOR HUGGING YOU LIKE THAT.

I SAW YOU WERE VERY NERVOUS, AND I THOUGHT YOU WERE HAVING A PANIC ATTACK.

YES...

THANK YOU SO MUCH, DORIAN.

PLEASE... LET ME STAY LIKE THIS FOR A FEW MOMENTS.

...

I DON'T THINK WILLIAM WILL BE HAPPY ABOUT IT.

...

SHOULD...?

SHOULD WE TALK ABOUT MY MARRIAGE?

YOUR MAJESTY!

ARE YOU HERE?

ARGH!

HURRY UP, HIDE, THIS COULD LOOK REALLY WEIRD!

UGH!

HI, YES, I'M HERE!

HE HE

WERE YOU LOOKING FOR ME?

OH, YES... YOU LEFT SO SUDDENLY, MAJESTY.

WE WERE WORRIED.

ARE YOU OK? SHOULD I ESCORT YOU BACK TO YOUR ROOM?

GLADLY, THANK YOU! I'M PERFECTLY FINE, HE HE!

...

CHAPTER 68

I'M TIRED, DAD! AND I'M HUNGRY! LET'S GO HOME AND EAT MAMA'S SOUP!

PATIENCE, ROBERT!

TOMORROW I'LL GO TO THE VILLAGE, AND I'M SURE PLENTY OF PEOPLE WILL WANT TO BUY A LOT OF FIREWOOD!

IT SEEMS THAT THE COLD WEATHER IS GONNA COME BACK IN THE NEXT COUPLE OF DAYS.

WELL, THAT'S WHY! IT'S SO COLD. WE SHOULD BE AT HOME DRINKING HOT SOUP!

UGH!

DADDY?! WHY HAVE YOU STOPPED ALL OF A SUDDEN?!

THERE'S...

THERE'S SOMEONE IN THE DARK...

AH, THAT'S TRUE...

IT'S A GIRL!

GOOD EVENING, LADY! ARE YOU ALL RIGHT?!

COME TO OUR SHELTER! WE'VE GOT HOT SOUP!

AND LOTS OF FIREWOOD!

DAD, LOOK AT HER HANDS!
THEY'RE BLOODY!
WHAT IF SHE'S A WITCH?!
I BET SHE'S EATEN A KID!
YOU'RE SCARED OF ME, THEN, YOU LITTLE INSECTS...
YOU DON'T LIKE WITCHES?
THEY SAID IT WAS TERRIFYING... THE WITCH'S EYES WERE FULLY RED...
YES, THE LUMBERJACK AND HIS SON SURVIVED BY SHEER LUCK!
WHAT? OF COURSE SHE DOESN'T EAT CHILDREN!

AND WHERE COULD WE FIND THE LUMBERJACK, GUYS?

WHAT ARE YOU DOING, AISHA?

DO YOU BELIEVE WHAT THEY'RE SAYING?

IT'S THE ONLY CLUE THAT WE'VE GOT AT THE MOMENT.

DID YOU HEAR THAT, MONICA? DANI IS EATING KIDS NOW.

CAN YOU PLEASE STOP STARING AND POINTING AT THEM, WILLIAM?

WE'RE SUPPOSED TO GO UNNOTICED.

...

HEY, DORIAN...

I'VE ALSO SEEN HER WITH RED EYES, AND IT CLEARLY WASN'T HER.

SHE WAS SORT OF POSSESSED.

THE REAL DANI'S STILL THERE AND WE CAN SAVE HER.

YOU HEARD THAT, RIGHT? DANI IS IN THE MOUNTAINS.

YES...

BUT IF THEY'RE ALREADY SCARED OF WITCHES, FLYING UP THERE WOULD BE DANGEROUS.

HOW CAN WE GET THERE WITHOUT BEING SEEN?

LEAVE IT TO ME AND MARK.

♪

AW! YOU LOOK SO HAPPY, MONICA!

I HAVEN'T HEARD YOU SING IN A WHILE!

INDEED, THREE YEARS TO BE PRECISE.

IT MUST BE THE HAPPINESS OF THE NEWLY MARRIED!

YEEEAH, SURE THING...

UGH!

HEY, DORIAN. ARE YOU OK, DUDE?

...

I'M SCARED...

DO YOU WANNA SEE SOMETHING REALLY COOL?

OH! A CRYSTAL BALL!

I GOT IT FROM MONICA'S SECRET LABORATORY!

DO YOU WANT ME TO TRY TO SEE THE FUTURE...?

EH, ARE YOU LISTENING TO ME?
DORIAN! WHAT ARE YOU LOOKING AT?
OH...!
WE'RE READY! LET'S GET TO IT!
HOW COOL, MONICA! YOU LOOK LIKE AN EXPERT ADVENTURER!
I KNOW! I'M AN ATHLETE AT HEART.
YOU'RE JUST WEARING PANTS.
...
DORIAN... WHAT'S WITH THAT FACE?
HUH?
DON'T BE SO OBVIOUS!
HOW ARE YOU DOING DOWN THERE? DO YOU NEED HELP?
NO! I CAN DO IT ON MY OWN. WHAT A PAIN!!
DON'T WORRY, DAMIEN! I WAS BORN FOR ADVENTURE!
IF YOU SAY SO...
ARGH!
WATCH YOUR STEP...
WILL, CAREFUL!

EH, BLOODY! DON'T BE SO SELFISH AND LEAVE SOME FOOD FOR CARLO!

BAD DRAGON, BAD DRAGON!

BLOODY? HIS NAME IS NOT BLOODY!

HMM?

HAVE YOU ALREADY GIVEN HIM A NAME?

YES! HIS NAME IS DONATO!

DONATO THE DRAGON!

DORIAN, THAT'S NOT A DRAGON NAME AT ALL!

EH? WELL, I THINK IT SUITS HIM...

BESIDES, HE LIKES IT. ISN'T THAT RIGHT, DONATO?

THAT'S TRUE, HE LIKES IT.

HUFF...

HA...

I'M SO TIRED...

HOW LONG HAVE WE BEEN CLIMBING?

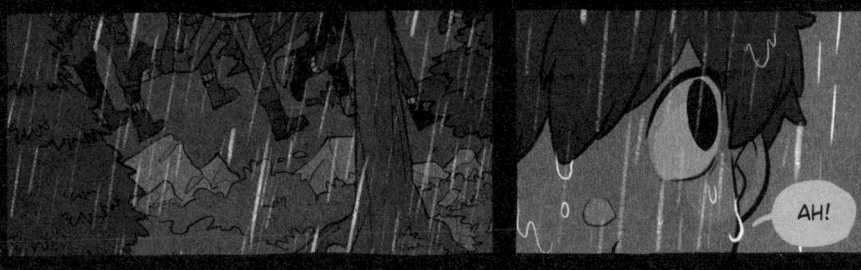

I TOLD YOU IT WAS GONNA RAIN!

AND WHAT DID YOU EXPECT US TO DO?!

WE HAD TO CLIMB THE MOUNTAIN!

IF ONLY DORIAN WASN'T SO SLOW!

I DO... WHAT I CAN.

STOP FIGHTING! WE NEED TO TAKE COVER!

AH!

LOOK, OVER THERE! IT'S THE LUMBERJACK'S SHELTER!

WE'VE ARRIVED!

IT SEEMS LIKE SOMETHING MUST HAVE SCARED THEM A LOT...

YEAH...

GOOD NEWS, THEN.

DANI IS HERE SOMEWHERE.

HUH... BUT... LOOK AT THE WINDOWS...

KNOCK KNOCK KNOCK

WHO'S THERE?!
ARE YOU THE WICKED WITCH OF THE MOUNTAINS?!
HUH? NO...?
AND IF I WAS, I WOULDN'T TELL YOU.
WE SEEK SHELTER. RAIN CAUGHT US IN THE MIDDLE OF NOWHERE!
...
WELCOME TO OUR HOME, THEN!
WE HAVE WARM SOUP!
AND PLENTY OF WOOD! COME AND WARM YOURSELVES BY THE FIRE!!
HOW COOL, WE HAVEN'T MET ANY HIKERS FOR A LONG TIME!
SINCE WE SAW THE WITCH...
THE RUMORS WERE TRUE, THEN... YOU SAW A WITCH...
THAT'S RIGHT, YOUNG MAN. MY SON AND I. SHE WAS TERRIFYING.

I WILL TELL YOU ABOUT IT.
BUT FIRST, MAKE YOURSELVES COMFORTABLE AND LET'S HAVE DINNER.
...
WERE YOU ALSO THINKING ABOUT DANI?
YES, IT'S JUST...
SHE'S THERE ALL ALONE.
...
YES... I'M WORRIED.
RIGHT NOW, SHE MUST BE OUT THERE IN THE RAIN, SURROUNDED BY COLD AND DARKNESS.
I DON'T THINK ANYTHING IS GONNA HAPPEN TO HER.
SHE HAS BECOME VERY STRONG.
YOU...
YOU'VE BEEN WITH HER, HAVEN'T YOU?
...
DURING THESE THREE YEARS?
EVERY SINGLE DAY.
WAITING FOR HER TO RECOVER.
TRYING TO GET A REACTION...
BUT... NOTHING.
I MISS HER SO MUCH.

ME TOO.

SOB
SOB

GUYS, GET INSIDE! LET'S HAVE DINNER!

AND SHUT THE DOOR, OR THE COLD GETS IN.

YES! I'M SORRY, MADAM!

THANK YOU SO MUCH! IT SMELLS SO GOOD!

YEAH, WELL... ABOUT WHAT YOU WERE ASKING, GUYS...

IT'S TRUE, WE SAW A WITCH IN THE MIDDLE OF THE MOUNTAIN, AT NIGHT...

SHE WAS COVERED IN BLOOD... SHE WAS TERRIFYING. SHE LOOKED LIKE A MONSTER.
WE HAVEN'T DARED TO LEAVE THE HOUSE AFTER DARK EVER SINCE.
INDEED... AND SHE THREATENED TO KILL US...
SHE SAID WE SHOULD BE PUNISHED FOR NOT BEING WITCHES
THAT'S ENOUGH!
EVERYONE TALKS ABOUT HER LIKE THAT, AND I... I MEAN... NOT ALL WITCHES ARE EVIL!
WE KNOW THAT, BOY.
WE ALWAYS READ "THE INSURGENT WITCH." THE POTIONS SECTION IS AWESOME!
WHAT'S "THE INSURGENT WITCH"?
WOW...
IT'S THE NEWSPAPER RUN BY WITCHES WHO ARE AGAINST WAR, YOUNG LADY!
I'M ALSO PRACTICING! EVEN THOUGH I CAN'T DO MUCH YET...
AH, SINCE YOU'RE TALKING ABOUT MAGIC SKILLS...
WE LEFT THE VILLAGE IN SUCH A HURRY THAT I ALMOST FORGOT...

LOOK! I'VE GOT A CRYSTAL BALL!

I HAVEN'T USED IT IN A LONG TIME. I HOPE IT'LL WORK! COME ON, SHOW ME HOW WE'RE GONNA RESCUE DANI!

AWESOME!

GOOD IDEA, NICO!

AH... I CAN SEE SOMETHING...

WOOO!! WHAT DO YOU SEE?!

EH?

IT SHOWED DORIAN WITH A PAIR OF SHORTS!!

WHAT A CRAPPY CRYSTAL BALL!!

EH?

REALLY?! IN SHORTS?!

PERHAPS THE BALL IS SUGGESTING THAT WE'LL SAVE DANI IN SUMMER?

WELL, IT'S DECEMBER NOW, SO...

SHORTS...

HOW WEIRD...

YAWN

COME ON, GET IN BED, EVERYONE! YOU MUST BE EXHAUSTED!

YOU CAN SLEEP IN THE BUNK BEDS!

THANK YOU SO MUCH!

WOULD IT BE POSSIBLE TO HAVE A PRIVATE ROOM FOR MY WIFE AND I? WE'RE NEWLY WED, YOU KNOW...?

AH...!

NO, NO, PLEASE DON'T BOTHER. SERIOUSLY! I PREFER TO SLEEP IN THE BUNK BEDS WITH THE OTHERS!
...
IT'S SETTLED: I'LL FIX YOU THE BEST ROOM OF THE HOUSE!
DARN YOU, WILLIAM! WHAT A SETUP!!
UGHHHH
FOLLOW ME, I'LL PREPARE THE BEDS.
HUH...?
THE BALL IS SHOWING ME SOMETHING...
BUT THIS...
THIS IS THE DAY DANI SAW DORIAN AT THE STAKE...
THE LAST TIME I SAW DANI...
AS SHE USED TO BE...
STOP!
WHAT KIND OF JOKE IS THIS?
WHY IS THE BALL SHOWING THE PAST...?

CHAPTER 69

I WANT THE UPPER BED!

ME TOO!

I WANT THIS ONE.

ARE YOU SERIOUS? DID YOU LEAVE ME OUT?

GOOD NIGHT, EVERYONE!

PILLOW FIGHT?!

HA-HA!

NICO, THAT'S NOT FUNNY! I ALMOST BUMPED AGAINST THE WOOD!

NOW THAT I THINK ABOUT IT, I DON'T WANNA SLEEP WITH A BUNCH OF KIDS...

THERE'S ANOTHER ROOM LIKE THIS ONE JUST ACROSS THE HALL.

I THINK I'M GONNA TAKE A BATH...

FINE, I'LL WAIT FOR YOU IN BED!

AH...
OH, HI, MONICA!
ON SECOND THOUGHT, I'M GONNA SLEEP IN DAMIEN'S ROOM.
I BELIEVE THERE WERE THREE FREE BEDS.
NOOO, WAIT!
PLEASE, WE HAVEN'T SPENT ONE NIGHT TOGETHER SINCE WE GOT MARRIED!
ALL RIGHT...
LOOKS LIKE IT'S STILL RAINING OUTSIDE...
I HOPE IT'LL STOP TOMORROW...
ARE YOU COMING TO BED?
IT'S LATE.
YES, I'M COMING!
HOW DID I END UP IN THIS SITUATION?
COME ON, MONICA. IT'S NOT A BIG DEAL.
YOU ONLY NEED TO SLEEP BY HIS SIDE.
IT WON'T BE THAT WEIRD.
WHEN WE WERE LITTLE, WE SLEPT TOGETHER PLENTY OF TIMES.
THERE'S NO DIFFERENCE NOW!
...

GOODNIGHT, WILL!
TURN OFF THE LIGHT, PLEASE!
OKAY...
WAAAA!!
WHAT ON EARTH ARE YOU DOING?!
I ONLY WANTED TO...KISS YOU GOODNIGHT.
DO YOU THINK THAT'S NORMAL?!
OF COURSE! YOU'RE MY WIFE, IT'S NORMAL!
SO WHAT?! IT'S NOT NORMAL IF I DON'T LIKE IT!!
WHAT'S GOING ON WITH YOU?
YOU'VE BEEN ACTING REALLY WEIRD SINCE WE GOT MARRIED.
YOU'RE MORE DISTANT THAN EVER, AND IT SHOULD BE THE OPPOSITE.
...

WHAT'S WRONG?!
PLEASE, MONICA... I DON'T UNDERSTAND.
WHAT HAVE I DONE TO YOU TO GET YOU SO MAD?
I'M NOT MAD AT YOU, WILL. IT'S NOT THAT...
IT'S JUST...
I THOUGHT BEING MARRIED TO YOU WOULD BE A LOT EASIER...
AFTER ALL, WE'VE KNOWN EACH OTHER ALL OUR LIVES,
AND I'VE ALWAYS KNOWN IT WAS GOING TO BE LIKE THIS...
OF COURSE. AND IT ISN'T WHAT YOU THOUGHT?
...
I LOVE YOU SO MUCH, WILL. I REALLY DO.
AND I'D LOVE TO SPEND MY LIFE WITH YOU, JUST AS IT WAS UNTIL NOW.
BUT I CAN'T LOVE YOU THE WAY YOU WANT ME TO.
I CAN'T BE YOUR WIFE.
WHAT?
WHAT DO YOU MEAN?

WELL, I MEAN THAT... I DON'T KNOW... MAYBE WE SHOULD ANNUL THE MARRIAGE...
SOMEHOW...?
WE CAN'T DO THAT!
OUR DUTY HAS ALWAYS BEEN THE UNION OF OUR KINGDOMS!
I WAS RAISED FOR THAT!!
WE CAN'T SPLIT UP NOW. THE PEOPLE WOULDN'T ACCEPT IT. IT'D BE A DISASTER!
WELL, THEN... I DON'T KNOW, I...
CAN'T WE SIMPLY PRETEND?
WH...?
WE'LL BE THE KING AND THE QUEEN THAT THEY ALL NEED!
BUT IT'S NOBODY'S BUSINESS IF WE'RE TOGETHER IN PRIVATE.
WHAT YOU'RE SAYING DOESN'T MAKE ANY SENSE.

IT WOULD BE WRONG...
COME ON, WILLIAM!
WHY ARE YOU ACTING LIKE THAT?
YOU HAVE TO DO YOUR JOB AS QUEEN!
WH...?
WHAT DO YOU WANT ME TO DO? TO KISS YOU EVEN WHEN WE'RE ALONE?!
IT'S!
OUR!
DUTY!
WELL, I CAN'T DO THAT.
BECAUSE I'M IN LOVE WITH DORIAN!

... WITH DORIAN...? THAT BRAT...?

UH... I'M IN LOVE WITH HIM!

I'M...!

AND I...

I WANT...

!

WILLIAM, WAIT!

...

UH... WHAT DID I JUST SAY?

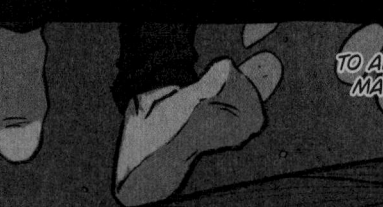

TO ANNUL THE MARRIAGE?

SHE'S IN LOVE WITH DORIAN?

IN LOVE?!

WHEN DID THAT HAPPEN?!

WHAT THE HELL IS WRONG WITH MONICA?!

CAN'T SHE UNDERSTAND THAT SHE'S THE QUEEN?!

WE NEED TO FULFILL OUR OBLIGATIONS!

THAT'S WHAT OUR PARENTS TOLD US!!

THAT'S WHAT THE WHOLE KINGDOM IS EXPECTING OF US!

WHY DOES SHE WANT TO THROW IT ALL AWAY...?!

WHY?!

ONLY BECAUSE SHE WANTS TO BE WITH DORIAN?

I DON'T GET IT.

WHAT DO YOU WANT, WILL?

IT'S MY DUTY TO MARRY MONICA.

TO BE HER HUSBAND.

TO BE THE KING.

WHAT'S ON YOUR MIND?

WHAT DO YOU WANT?

...

WHY DID I END UP HERE?!

THE QUEEN!

DORIAN, GET UP!

WHAT'S GOING ON, WILLIAM...? HAVE YOU WET THE BED AGAIN...?

IT'S YOUR SISTER, DORIAN! SHE'S HERE!

WHAT...?

DANI...!
WHERE IS SHE?!
THERE, BY THE WINDOW!
DANI...! WHERE...?
AH...!
DANI...

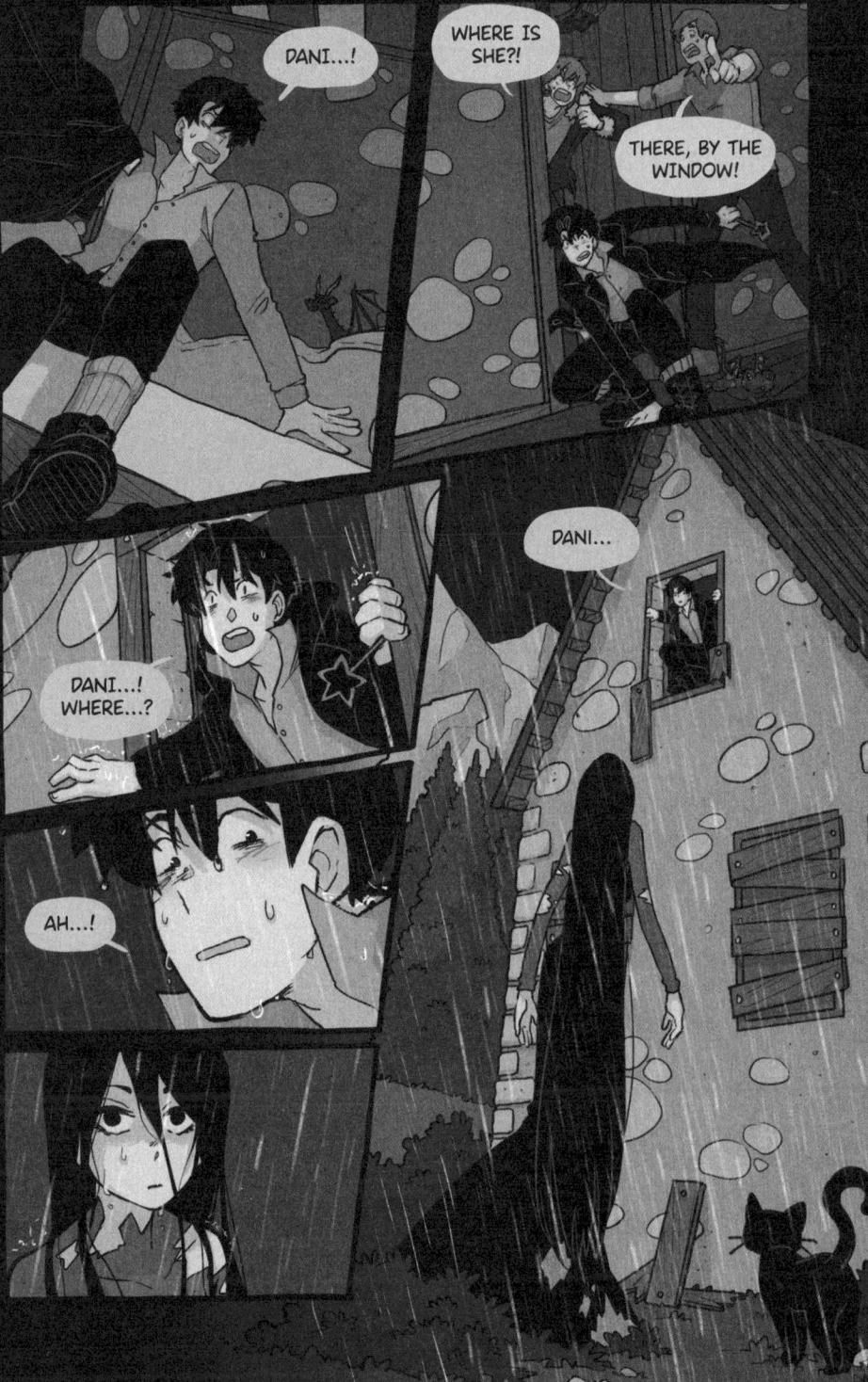

WOW... IT LOOKS LIKE THERE'S PLENTY OF PEOPLE IN THIS HOUSE...

GOOD...

KILL THEM.

LET ONLY ONE LIVE.

IT'LL BE GOOD...

...

ALL RIGHT.

DANI!

IT'S ME, DORIAN!

DANI, SAY SOMETHING!

WHAT'S GOING ON?

WHY ARE YOU BEING SO LOUD?!

IT'S YOUR SISTER!!

WHAT?!

DORIAN...

I THINK SHE...

SHE CAN'T RECOGNIZE ME...

I DON'T KNOW WHAT SORT OF REACTION I WAS EXPECTING FROM HER, BUT...

SHE ISN'T RESPONDING AT ALL.

THAT...

WAKE UP!

I'M SORRY IT TOOK ME SO LONG TO COME FOR YOU, DANI, I...!

I SHOULD HAVE BEEN BY YOUR SIDE!

BUT I'M BEGGING YOU, SAY SOMETHING!

RESPOND! DANI...!

CHANGE OF PLANS...

...

WHAT DO YOU WANT?

THAT GUY IS VERY POWERFUL... AND HIS DESPAIR... IS DELICIOUS.

I NEED MORE OF THAT.

... OKAY.

AH...

WHAT'S GOING ON?! WHAT'S ALL THAT NOISE?!

MUM, IT'S THE WITCH! THE WITCH IS BACK!

GOOD, GOOD... THIS WILL DO...

DON'T WORRY, WE WON'T LET HER HURT YOU!

WHAT...?

WHOAAAH!
RUN, GET OUT OF THE HOUSE!
MARK, TAKE THE CHILD!
DORIAN! WHAT'S GOING ON?!
WHY ARE YOU DOING THIS?
GOODBYE.
NO...
DON'T GO...
DANI, WAIT!

DANI... UH...
DON'T... PLEASE...
THAT'S NOT MY DANI!
COME BACK!
TSK!
DORIAN! WHAT ON EARTH ARE YOU DOING?!
I'M FOLLOWING HER!
I'LL BRING HER BACK, I PROMISE!
YOU STAY HERE!
DON'T YOU DARE FOLLOW ME. IT'S TOO DANGEROUS!
WHAT ARE YOU TALKING ABOUT, IDIOT?!
YOU CAN'T GO BY YOURSELF!
DORIAN!

NICO, DON'T JUST STAND THERE! WE NEED TO GET OUT OF HERE, HURRY!
DORIAN RAN OFF AFTER DANI! SHE DIDN'T RECOGNIZE HIM! SHE'S GONNA HURT HIM, MARK!
DORIAN'S IN DANGER!
MARK! ARE YOU OK?!
YES! BUT DORIAN'S GONE!
I KNOW. IT WAS IMPOSSIBLE NOT TO SEE HIM TAKE OFF WITH THE DRAGONS.
ALL RIGHT, OUT OF THE WAY, EVERYONE!
I THINK I CAN STOP THE FIRE.
!
WAIT, DAMIEN! WHERE'S MONICA?!

I HOPE... HE'LL FORGIVE ME...
WAS I TOO DIRECT?
...?
IS IT TRUE, THEN?
AM I IN LOVE WITH DORIAN?
...
WHEN EVERYTHING GOES BACK TO NORMAL...
ONCE DANI'S WITH US AGAIN...
I'LL TELL HIM...
HUH?
DOES IT SMELL LIKE SMOKE?
OH NO.
FIRE! IT'S PURPLE FIRE!
WHAT THE...?!
I CAN ONLY GET OUT THROUGH THE WINDOW, BUT IT'S TOO HIGH...!
I NEED A BROOM, OR...!
OH!
NO WAY.

DANI! DORIAN, WAIT!
MONICA!
DAMIEN!
ARE YOU ALL RIGHT?! ARE YOU HURT?!
I'M OK, BUT DORIAN...!
I'M GONNA FIND A BROOM AND COME FOR YOU!
WAIT, TAKE TWO! TAKE TWO BROOMS!
TWO BROOMS...?
OF COURSE, TWO BROOMS!
WAIT, WHAT? WHY TWO?

YES. LET'S GO.
ARE YOU READY?
WAIT, DAMIEN!
WAIT, MONICA! YOU TWO!
HEY! DON'T LEAVE LIKE THAT!
AAAND THEY'RE ALL GONE. SIGH, I HATE WITCHES.
BUT YOU'RE A WITCH TOO, NICO.
LOOK, MUM! THEY'RE FLYING!!
ARE YOU DOING OK?
Y...YES! I HAVEN'T BEEN ON A BROOM IN A LONG TIME!
DON'T GO... I CAN'T LOSE YOU BOTH...

WE CAN'T JUST SIT HERE AND WAIT!
WE MUST HELP THEM!
I AGREE WITH WILL, FOR ONCE!
THEY MIGHT NEED US!
YES, WE MUST HELP DORIAN!
WHERE DID YOU FIND THAT, AISHA?!
DON'T YOU DARE TOUCH DANI WITH IT!
GUYS... BE CAREFUL.
YES, MUCH STRENGTH TO YOU!
GOOD LUCK, WITCHES!
ARE THEY ALSO GONNA FLY ON A BROOM, MUMMY?
THANK YOU SO MUCH FOR EVERYTHING.
AND WE'RE SORRY FOR WHAT HAPPENED.
LATER WE'LL COME BACK TO FIX THE SHELTER. I PROMISE!

I WON'T LET YOU RUN AWAY LIKE THIS!
YOU HEAR ME?!
WHERE ARE YOU GOING?!
DANI, STOP!
UGH!
LISTEN TO ME!
AH!

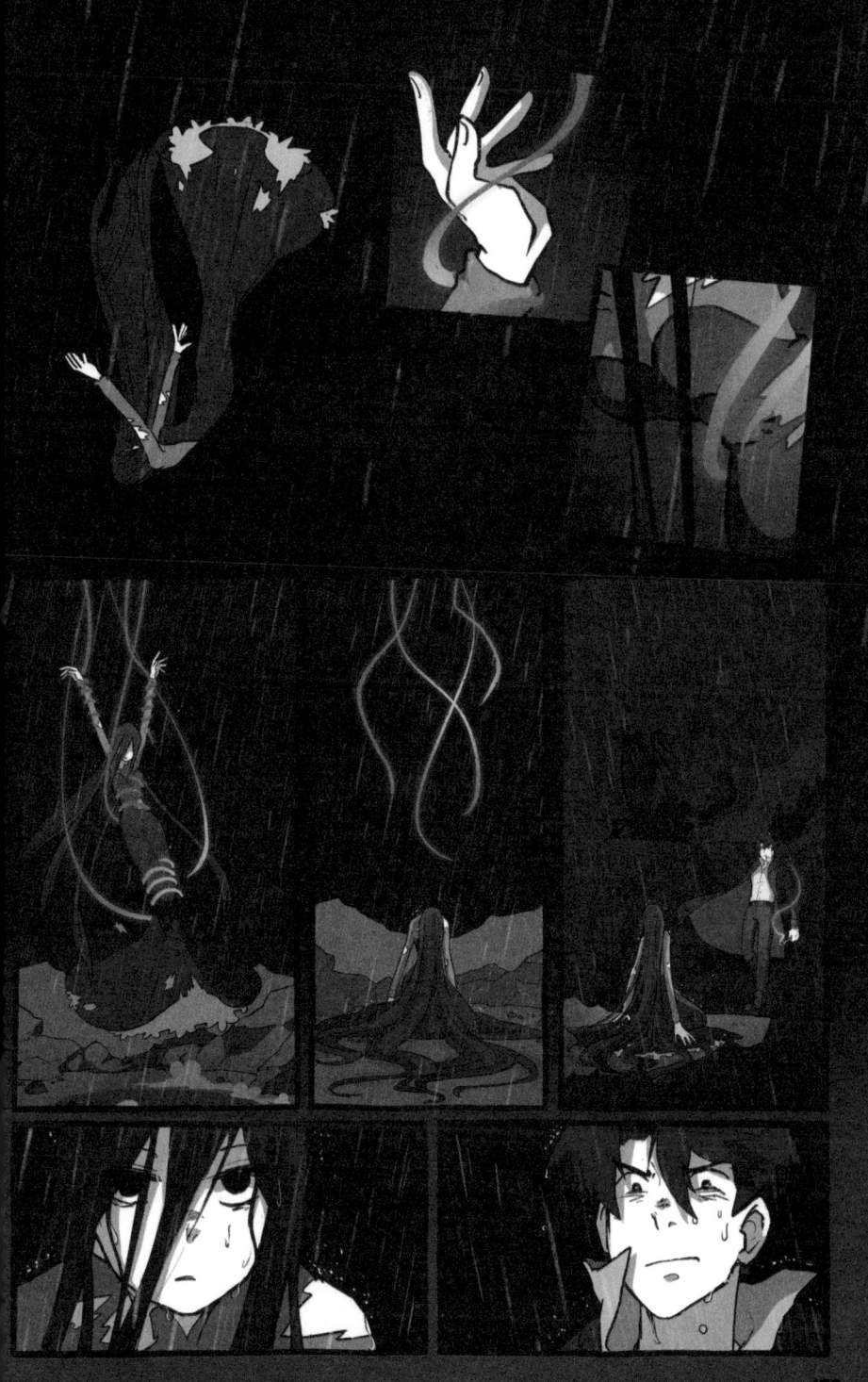

DANI, LOOK AT ME!

IT'S ME, DORIAN!

I'M YOUR BROTHER!

LOOK CLOSELY, WE LOOK A LOT LIKE EACH OTHER!

... BROTHER?

YES, IT'S ME!

DO YOU REMEMBER ME NOW?!

UGH...

COME ON, GET UP. I WILL TAKE YOU TO THE OTHERS.

TOGETHER, WE WILL FIND A WAY FOR YOU TO GET BETTER.

NO...

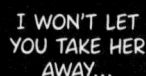
I WON'T LET YOU TAKE HER AWAY...

WHEW, YOU'VE ALSO GROWN UP A LOT!

YOU'RE AS TALL AS NICO! OR MAYBE A BIT MORE...?

UH...

DANI?

HUH?

WHAT IS GOING ON?!
WHAT ARE YOU DOING?!
DA...!
...NI...
UH...
RED EYES.
FOCUS, DORIAN.
WHAT HAVE YOU READ ABOUT RED EYES?

NOT THIS...

OR THIS...

NO, THIS ISN'T USEFUL...

BUT THERE'S SOMETHING...

DEEP DOWN...

HEY, DORIAN...

I REMEMBER SOMETHING...

I'VE ALSO SEEN HER WITH RED EYES, AND IT CLEARLY WASN'T HER.

SHE WAS SORT OF POSSESSED.

BOOM

SHE'S POSSESSED! AN EVIL SPIRIT LIES WITHIN HER...

MONICA WAS RIGHT.

DANI HASN'T BECOME EVIL!

AND I KNOW HOW TO GET IT OUT!

YOU'LL SEE!
I'LL SET MY SISTER FREE!
ARE YOU TALKING TO ME?
AH!

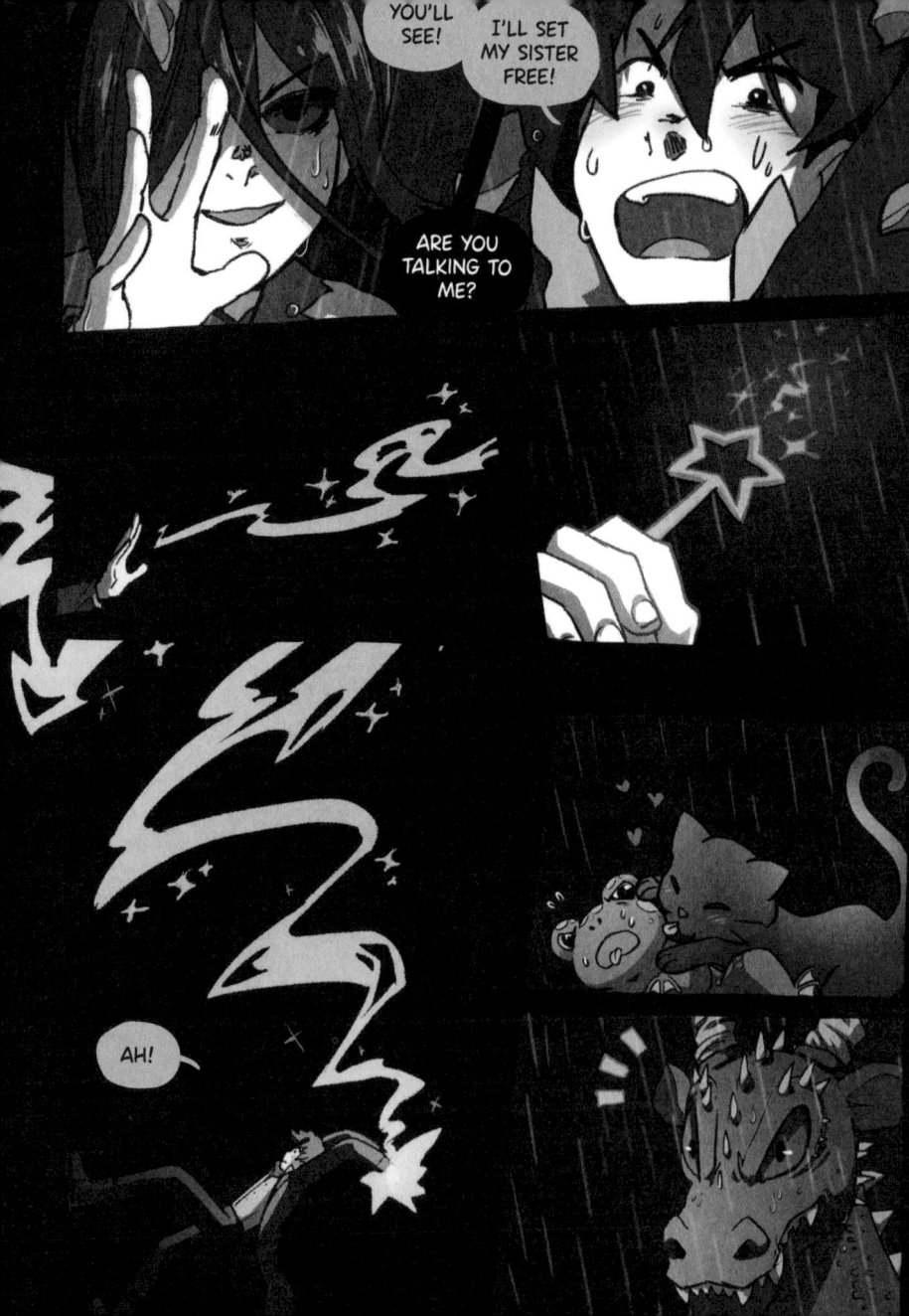

POW
ADORABLE...
THAT EXPRESSION IS ADORABLE...
UGH...
...ELSE.
OH NO.
NO WAY.
I DIDN'T SEE IT COMING...
I NEED TO TRY SOMETHING...

!
ROOAAARR
DONATO, STOP!
LEAVE HER ALONE!
BOOM
DONATO!
NO.
NO.
NO.
NO.
PLEASE. NO.
THIS ISN'T REAL.
NO.
NO.

UH...
NO...
NO...
DONATO... NO...
I'M SORRY!
YOU'LL BE FINE, LITTLE ONE.
THIS IS MY FAULT... I TOOK YOU ALL THE WAY HERE.
I SHOULD HAVE KEPT YOU SAFE, ALL OF YOU.
I PROMISE, YOU'LL BE FINE. I'M SORRY.
MMM... DELICIOUS...
YES, IT'S GETTING BETTER...
DORIAN!

IT LOOKS LIKE WE'VE ARRIVED JUST IN TIME...

ARE YOU OK?! YOU'RE BLEEDING!

!

WHAT HAPPENED TO THE DRAGON?!

... UH...

NO.

WAIT. NO...!

LOOKS LIKE DORIAN'S IN TROUBLE.

WE'RE THE ONES IN TROUBLE! DANI IS COMING THIS WAY!

STAY AWAY, DANI!

MONICA, GO GET DORIAN!

YES!

WE NEED TO GET HIM OUT OF HERE RIGHT NOW.

THE BARRIER WON'T HOLD FOR MUCH LONGER!

...THEY SEEM TO HAVE EVERYTHING UNDER CONTROL...

WHAT DO YOU THINK, CARLO?

YOU WERE RIGHT ABOUT DANI!

SHE'S NOT EVIL OR CRAZY!

DORIAN!

DORIAN!

I DISCOVERED SHE'S JUST POS--

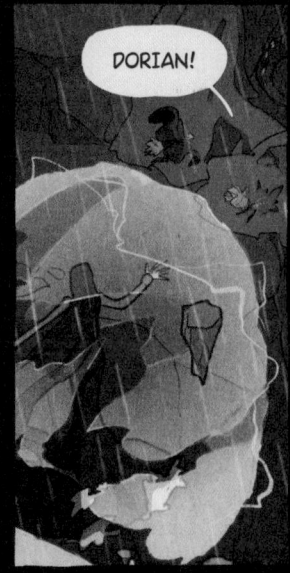

YOU TALK TOO MUCH, KID.
YOU SHOULD KEEP OUR LITTLE SECRET.
IS HE OKAY?!
I...I DON'T KNOW! HE'S BREATHING... BUT I THINK HE'S UNCONSCIOUS!
UGH...
WHOAA!
DAMIEN!
YES... PERFECT...
NOW I FEEL STRONGER... MORE ALIVE...
CHAOS GIVES ME STRENGTH...
TURN HER INTO A FROG OR A MOUSE OR...!
IT'S DAMIEN, YOUR BROTHER! REMEMBER!
DAMIEN, DO ONE OF YOUR SPELLS!
YES! MY SPECIALTY! I'LL TURN YOU INTO AN INSIGNIFICANT...

...GIANT SNAKE?!
AAARGH!
I SAID A MOUSE!
IT WAS SUPPOSED TO BE A NORMAL-SIZED SNAKE!
WHY IS IT SO BIG?! I DON'T GET IT!
TURN IT INTO DANI AGAIN, QUICK!
YES, RIGHT AWAY!
BUT FIRST...
RUN!
WAAAAAH!

UGH...
WHEW...
COLORED LIGHTS KEEP APPEARING BEHIND THOSE MOUNTAINS.
THEY SHOULDN'T BE TOO FAR.
YES... THOSE FIREWORKS ARE UNMISTAKABLE...
I CAN'T TAKE IT ANYMORE... WHERE ARE THEY...?
YOU RAN TOO FAST, MAJESTY.
MONICA... DAMIEN... WHERE ARE YOU...?
AH!
WHAT'S THAT...?
A MONSTER?!
AND IT'S CHASING MONICA AND DAMIEN!
UGH!

HEY, WILLIAM!
I'M BORROWING THIS. IT'S AN EMERGENCY!
WILLIAM, COME BACK HERE!
WHAT'S GOING ON, AISHA?
IT'S WILLIAM! HE'S GOING AFTER A GIANT SNAKE!!
WHAT?
DANI'S OUT OF CONTROL!
AND SHE'S STILL FLYING!
HOW IS SHE FLYING WITHOUT A BROOM?!
I HAVE NO CLUE! SHE'S FREAKING POWERFUL!
QUICK, DAMIEN, BRING HER BACK TO HER NORMAL SHAPE!
AT LEAST THIS WAY WE WON'T END UP IN HER STOMACH!
AS SOON AS SHE GIVES US A BREAK...!

AH!
OVER THERE!
A CAVE?!
OF COURSE! WE'LL HIDE IN THERE FOR A LITTLE WHILE!
SNAKE-DANI IS TOO BIG TO FIT!
PERFECT...
I'M HERE...JUST IN TIME...
DAMIEN, NOW!
HEY, YOU--HORRIBLE CREATURE!
STAY AWAY FROM MY BELOVED AND MY BEST FRIEND!
I, KING WILLIAM...

...WILL PUNISH YOU!
NO, WILLIAM, WAIT!
THAT'S DA--

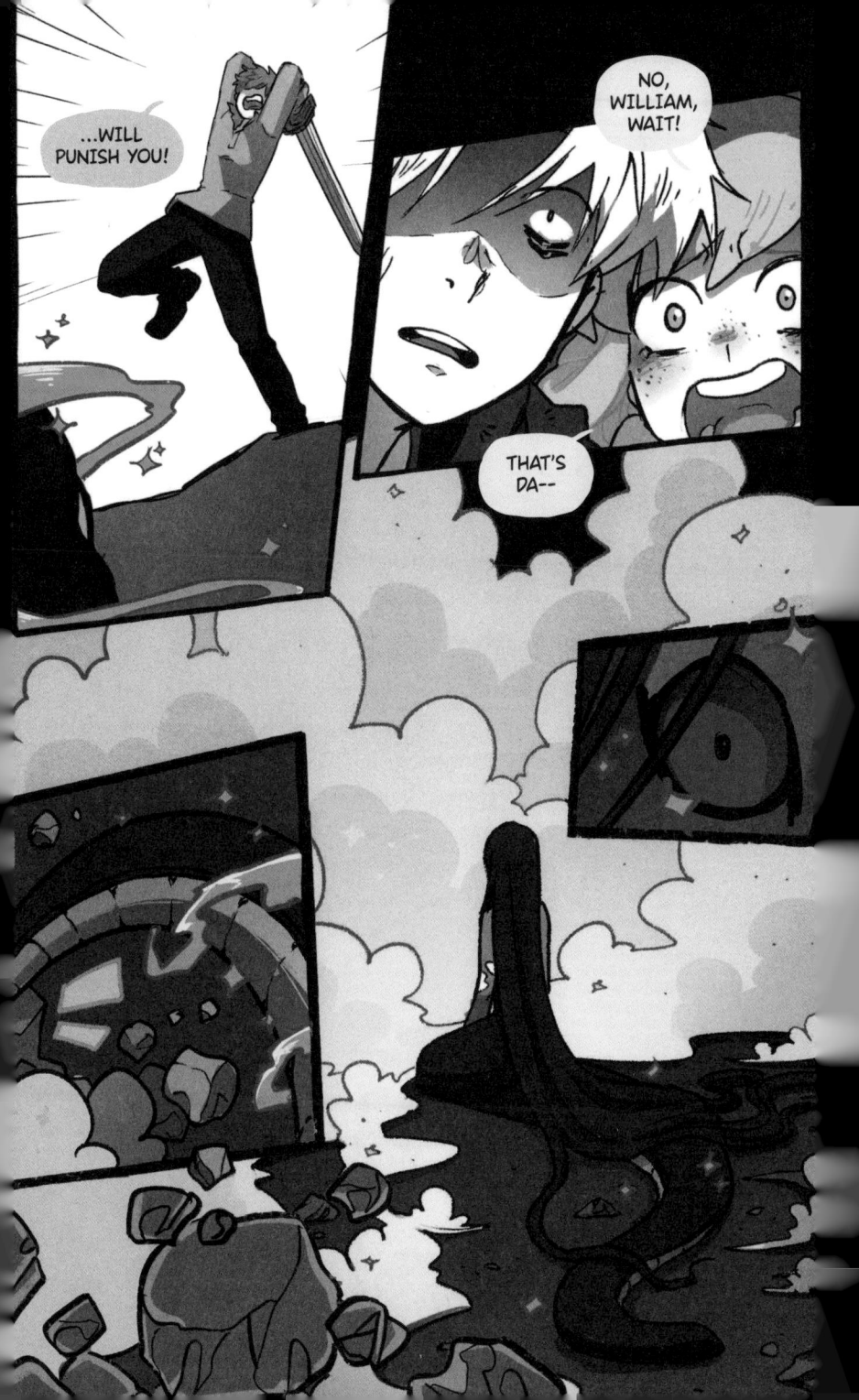

WHAT HAPPENED?!
WHERE'S KING WILLIAM?
!
AH... DANI'S OVER THERE!
WILLIAM!! ARE YOU THERE?!
OH NO... TELL ME HE'S OKAY...
MAJESTY!
WHERE IS SHE GOING?
...
WE SHOULD FOLLOW HER!
WHAT ABOUT WILLIAM? WHERE IS HE?

WE'RE OVER HERE!
MONICA!! ARE YOU OK?!
YES, WE'RE FINE!
BUT YOU MUST HURRY TO HELP DORIAN. I THINK DANI HURT HIM.
HE FAINTED.
SHE WOULDN'T HURT HIM.
WE CAN'T BE SURE.
ALSO, DORIAN SEEMS TO HAVE FOUND OUT SOMETHING! WHEN I SAW HIM HE LOOKED SO HAPPY!
GREAT.
OH, AND NICO...
BE CAREFUL. I BELIEVE IN YOU!
TREAD CAREFULLY, QUEEN MONICA.
THAT'S MY LINE.
I WON'T BE ABLE TO BE YOUR BODYGUARD THIS TIME.
DON'T WORRY ABOUT ME. I CAN TAKE CARE OF MYSELF.

WILL YOU BE FINE?

YES...

... PERFECTLY WELL.

HOW COULD YOU EVEN THINK OF DOING SUCH A THING?! ARE YOU OUT OF YOUR MIND, WILL?!

WE'RE ALIVE BY A MIRACLE! YOU COULD HAVE DIED!

SORRY FOR TRYING TO SAVE YOU FROM A TERRIFYING AND LETHAL MONSTER!

BUT THAT'S NOT A MONSTER, THAT'S DANI! WE'VE COME HERE TO SAVE HER! REMEMBER?

YOU ALWAYS ACT WITHOUT THINKING!

HOW COULD I KNOW THAT THING WAS DANI?!

HE'S KINDA RIGHT...

... IT DOESN'T MATTER.

EITHER WAY, JUMPING ON A MONSTER LIKE THAT IS CRAZY.
WHA...?!
YOU TWO WOULD HAVE DONE EXACTLY THE SAME!
YOU FLEW AWAY TO GO AFTER DORIAN AND DANI WITHOUT EVEN THINKING!
YOU DON'T GET HOW DANGEROUS THIS IS, WILL.
STAY OUT OF IT.
BUT WE'RE WITCHES!
YOU'RE NOT!
...
ALL RIGHT, I GOT IT!
NOBODY NEEDS ME ANYMORE!
WHAAAT?!
I DIDN'T SAY THAT, WILL, I...
NEVER MIND. WHAT MATTERS NOW IS TO GET OUT OF HERE.
WHERE'S MY WAND?

WILL...!

I'M USELESS...

OH, COME ON! ENOUGH WITH THE TANTRUM!

I NEVER SAID YOU'RE USELESS, WILL!

...

NO... YOU'RE NOT USELESS, WILL!

I THINK I WENT TOO FAR WITH HIM...

...

I KNOW IT'S DANGEROUS.

DANI'S UNLEASHED.

AND YOU TWO...

THAT'S WHY I WAS TERRIFIED SOMETHING BAD WOULD HAPPEN TO YOU.

I THOUGHT I WAS GONNA LOSE YOU.

THAT'S WHY I ACTED WITHOUT THINKING... BUT WHAT DID YOU EXPECT ME TO DO?

BUT IT'S CLEAR NOW...

EVERY SINGLE TIME I TRY TO FULFILL MY DUTY, I JUST MANAGE TO MESS THINGS UP...

...AND ANNOY THE BOTH OF YOU.

WILL...
WE'LL FIND A WAY...TO MAKE THINGS RIGHT.
WE'LL REIGN TOGETHER.
AND WE'LL DO IT TO THE BEST OF OUR ABILITIES.
I WON'T LEAVE YOU ALONE.
I'VE TOLD YOU BEFORE AND I'M TELLING YOU NOW.
I LOVE YOU, AND I'LL ALWAYS BE BY YOUR SIDE.
I'M SORRY I YELLED AT YOU... I WAS CONFUSED.
WELL, I STILL AM.
BUT I ALSO WANNA DO THINGS RIGHT.
EVEN THOUGH I'M NOT ENTIRELY SURE WHAT "RIGHT" MEANS...
I FEEL LIKE A THIRD WHEEL HERE...
WHERE'S THE WAND...?
...?

DAMIEN.
HUH?
...
WHAT? WHAT IS IT?
YOU'RE NOT LEAVING EITHER, ARE YOU?
WILL WE STILL BE FRIENDS, THE THREE OF US?
WAIT, WHAT?
WHAT DO YOU MEAN, "FRIENDS"?
YOU TWO AREN'T FRIENDS...
WELL, ACTUALLY, WE ARE.
MONICA JUST TOLD ME SHE ONLY WANTS TO BE MY FAKE WIFE.
DON'T TELL ANYONE THOUGH!

IN PUBLIC WE WILL BE KING AND QUEEN.
BUT IN PRIVATE WE WON'T HAVE ANY KIND OF ROMANTIC RELATIONSHIP.
PEOPLE WOULDN'T UNDERSTAND IT, BUT THAT'S THE ONLY WAY IT CAN WORK!
TRUE.
UH... DAMIEN...
YOU'VE BEEN VERY QUIET.
HUH?
DO YOU THINK THIS IS BAD?
NO.
I BELIEVE YOU SHOULD NEVER DO SOMETHING YOU'RE NOT COMFORTABLE WITH.
ACTUALLY, I'VE ALWAYS THOUGHT THAT YOUR MARRIAGE OPPRESSED YOU.
I GUESS...I'M SURPRISED YOU ALSO FEEL THAT WAY.
AWESOME. WELL, LET'S GET OUT OF HERE NOW!

YOUR WAND MUST BE BURIED, DAMIEN!
YOU CAN HELP ME WITH THIS, WILL!
LIFT THE HEAVIER ROCKS. YOU'RE STRONGER THAN US.
NICE!
...
BOOOM

WHOA... COOL...

WELL, YEAH... HE'S QUITE IMPRESSIVE...

THANK YOU SO MUCH, DAMIEN! YOU RULE!

COME ON, YOU GUYS! THE OTHERS NEED OUR HELP!

WHY DID WILLIAM LOOK AT ME THAT WAY? WHAT IS THAT IDIOT THINKING?

AAAARGH, I'M THE REAL IDIOT HERE. I'M WAY TOO HAPPY.

NO, NO, NO, DAMIEN. NOW IS NOT THE TIME.

YOUR CLUMSY SIBLINGS NEED TO BE RESCUED BEFORE THEY GET HURT FOR REAL.

KEEP A CLEAR HEAD!

TAKE IT, DAMIEN!

AH!

HURRY UP, WILL! GET ON MY BROOM!

DON'T WORRY, I'LL GET ON DAMIEN'S BROOM. IT'S NOT THE FIRST TIME HE'S TAKEN ME AS A COPILOT!

CLEAR HEAD. CLEAR HEAD.

!

WHILE WE'RE FLYING YOU CAN GIVE ME LOVE ADVICE, DAMIEN.
NOW THAT I'M SINGLE AGAIN.
IF YOU DON'T SHUT UP, I'LL THROW YOU OFF THE BROOM, YOU FOOL.
DAMIEN. I WANT TO TELL YOU SOMETHING BEFORE WE CONFRONT DANI AGAIN.
I BROUGHT THIS TO USE IN CASE IT IS NECESSARY.
IT'S... THE POTION I USED ON YOUR MOTHER, YES.
TO END HER MAGICAL POWERS FOREVER.
I CAN THROW IT AWAY IF YOU WANT. I'M NOT SURE IF I WAS RIGHT TO BRING IT.
NO, KEEP IT.
JUST IN CASE.

UGH...

THIS STUPID BODY ONCE AGAIN...

I NEED TO GAIN STRENGTH...OR THAT SPOILED BRAT WON'T LET ME USE HERS...

AH! YOU FINALLY APPEARED!

ABOUT TIME!

HAVEN'T YOU NOTICED?!

?

LOOK, KILL THEM ALL AND LET'S GET OUT OF HERE.

I WAS DOING SO WELL, BEING A GIANT SNAKE...

HEY... THEY'RE AFTER YOU!

I'M BORED OUT OF MY HEAD. THESE PEOPLE ARE TIRING.

... ALL RIGHT.

DANI...

AH! LOOK! DORIAN'S OVER THERE!

SHE SAW US!

TRUE. I HOPE HE'S FIN--

UGH!

MARK!
WHA...?!
DANI, LEAVE HIM ALONE!
DANI! LISTEN!
UH...
AISHA, GO AND WAKE UP DORIAN!
NO! I WON'T LEAVE HIM!
I WON'T LET YOU ATTACK DANI!
...
WAKING DORIAN IS THE BEST OPTION WE HAVE. HE'LL KNOW HOW TO HANDLE THIS!
OKAY! BUT KEEP HER DISTRACTED, NICO, OR I SWEAR I...!
OF COURSE!
DANI...
THIS SITUATION BRINGS SOME MEMORIES BACK...
HAVE YOU INTOXICATED YOURSELF WITH A FAILED LOVE POTION?
LOVE POTION...?

IF YOU'RE TRYING TO HURT ME, YOU'RE NOT DOING A GREAT JOB.
YOU'RE STILL NOT VERY STRONG!
YOU SHOULD USE OTHER METHODS.
DO IT.
DANI...?!
WAIT, DANI, IT WAS A JOKE...!
NO!

...
MARK, ARE YOU...?
YES, I'M FINE.
BY THE SKIN OF MY TEETH.
THANKS, NICO.
WHAT WERE YOU THINKING?! WERE YOU SERIOUSLY ABOUT TO BLOW MARK'S HEAD UP, DANI?!
WHO?
WHAT DO YOU MEAN, WHO?!
MARK!
CAN'T YOU REMEMBER HIM?! DON'T TELL ME YOU CAN'T EVEN REMEMBER ME; I'VE BEEN BY YOUR SIDE ALL THIS TIME!
AH...?
YES... NICO.
YOU'VE BETRAYED ME.
NO.

BECAUSE HE TELLS ME TO DO IT.
WHAT DO YOU MEAN? WHAT'S HAPPENING TO YOU?
YOUR MOTHER IS NO LONGER HERE TO BOSS YOU AROUND.
WHY ARE YOU DOING THIS?
WHY WERE YOU GONNA KILL MARK?
HE?
WHO ARE YOU TALK...?
!

DON'T TELL ME...

GUYS, ARE YOU ALL OKA--

AAAAAAAARGH!

DORIAN!

WHAT A MOMENT TO FALL FLAT ON YOUR FACE, DORIAN!

DANI...!

... YES... OKAY...

HELP ME CATCH HER!

I KNOW HOW TO BRING HER BACK!
BUT I NEED A WAND!
HEY, WAIT, NO!
IT'S THE CAT, DORIAN!
THE CAT!
UH...!
HEY, YOU TWO! QUIT THE REUNION AND DON'T LET THE CAT GET AWAY!
HUH?
I GOT YOU!
WE'VE GOT THE CAT, NICO. WHAT ARE WE GONNA DO WITH IT?
PERFECT!

I FIGURED IT OUT. THERE'S A SPIRIT INSIDE HER!
HELP ME HOLD HER!
NO, DORIAN, YOU'RE WRONG. THE SPIRIT IS...!
AH!
DAMIEN, QUICK, THE WAND!
WHAT'S ALL THIS MESS?!
EVERYONE'S HERE!
THEY'VE GOT DANI!
ARE YOU OKAY, DORIAN?
YES!
HEY, WAIT...!
DAMIEN, PLEASE! THE WAND!
HERE, DORIAN!
I HOPE YOU KNOW WHAT YOU'RE DOING!
ALWAYS!

LET'S DO IT, AT LAST...!

STOP, DORIAN!

LISTEN TO ME NOW! LEAVE DANI ALONE!

THE SPIRIT THAT CONTROLS HER IS INSIDE THE BODY OF THE CAT!

WHAT...?

AH?

LOOK AT ITS EYES...!

NICO?

DANI?

AH... I THINK...
I THINK I'VE BEEN HERE BEFORE.
HUH?
THE SHELTER...
WHEN DID WE RETURN?
WHAT...?
WHAT WAS I DOING OUT THERE?
I FEEL LIKE I JUST WOKE UP FROM A DREAM...
DO YOU THINK DORIAN WILL COME BACK?
BAH, WHO CARES!
!
WITH A BIT OF LUCK HE AND DANI WILL KILL EACH OTHER!
HAHAHA, DAMN, NICO, YOU'RE SO MEAN!
ARE THEY TALKING ABOUT ME...?
YOU KNOW THOSE TWO HAVEN'T GIVEN US ANYTHING BUT PROBLEMS SINCE THEIR ARRIVAL.
IT SEEMS LIKE THEY ARE CURSED!
I THINK THEY ARE INDEED!
HOW SICK.
AND ON TOP OF THAT, DORIAN IS SUCH A PAIN. I NEVER LIKED HIM ANYWAY.

DANI WAS SO COOL. IT'S SUCH A SHAME THAT SHE WENT CRAZY!

WHATEVER, THERE'S NOTHING TO DO!

YES, IT LOOKS LIKE EVERYTHING'S GOING GREAT.

WE'VE KILLED TWO BIRDS WITH ONE STONE AND WITHOUT GETTING OUR HANDS DIRTY.

I WANT TO GO BACK TO THE PALACE. I NEVER THOUGHT MY FAMILY WOULD PERSECUTE ME FOR SO LONG! WHAT A NIGHTMARE!

THERE'S A REASON WHY I GOT OUT OF THERE.

YEAH, IT MUST BE HARD TO BE BLOOD BOUND TO SUCH TWISTED PEOPLE.

AH, DORIAN...

DORIAN! WHAT ARE YOU DOING HERE?

DID YOU ACTUALLY HEAR...?

THIS IS STUPID. IT MAKES NO SENSE.

I DON'T KNOW WHO YOU ARE, BUT YOU'RE NOT MY FRIENDS.

HMM... I'D SAY THIS DOOR WASN'T HERE BEFORE...

WHERE ARE YOU GOING, DORIAN?

I'M LOOKING FOR DANI.

SOMETHING TELLS ME SHE'S REALLY CLOSE...

... WHO'S THAT?

HMM...?

AH... YOU.

HI, SON.

IT'S BEEN A LONG TIME.

I'M GLAD TO SEE YOU'VE GROWN UP...

YOU RESEMBLE ME A LOT!

EVEN THOUGH I WOULD NEVER HAVE BETRAYED MY OWN FAMILY TO THE POINT OF KILLING MY FATHER.

YOU'VE GOT SOME AUDACITY, DORIAN...

IN THE END, YOU'RE THE MOST TWISTED AMONG US...

HUH?

I'VE GOT NO TIME FOR SUCH SILLINESS.

I KNOW YOU'RE NOT MY REAL FATHER, AND ALL OF THIS SOUNDS LIKE A BAD JOKE.

I NEED TO FIND DANI. LEAVE ME ALONE.

WHERE DO YOU THINK YOU'RE GOING?! MURDERER!

YOU'VE KILLED ME! YOU'LL NEVER FIND DANI!

HEY...

HELLO, SWEETHEART...

STOP IT, SERIOUSLY. THE MORE YOU TRY, THE MORE I REMEMBER THIS PLACE.

IT'S NOT THE FIRST TIME YOU TRIED TO SCARE ME.

YOU'RE NOT MY REAL MOTHER.

RIGHT, YOUR MOTHER IS ALONE, LOCKED UP IN THAT COLD PALACE, SURROUNDED BY ENEMIES AND DEPRIVED OF HER POWERS.

YOU'VE ABANDONED HER. HAVEN'T YOU, DORIAN?

THAT'S NOT TRUE! YOU DON'T KNOW ME!

YOU THINK YOU CAN LOOK THROUGH ME,

THAT YOU CAN CONTROL AND TERRIFY ME WITH CHEAP TRICKS.

IT'S SIMPLE, THOUGH. YOU DON'T KNOW A SINGLE THING. I WON'T ABANDON MY MOTHER.

OR DANI.

I DON'T KNOW HOW I ENDED UP HERE, BUT I REMEMBER I CAME FOR HER.

I'LL GET HER OUT OF THIS PLACE, AND WE'LL BE TOGETHER AGAIN, AS A FAMILY. ALL OF US.

STOP FOLLOWING ME.

DORIAN, DON'T GET DISTRACTED. DANI'S PROBABLY TRAPPED SOMEWHERE.

I NEED TO GET HER OUT OF HERE, NO MATTER WHAT.

AH!

DANI!

... DORIAN?

WAAAH!

WHAT HAPPENED?

I'M SO GLAD YOU'RE HERE! WE NEED TO DO SOMETHING!

EVERYTHING... EVERYTHING'S GOING WRONG, DORIAN. WE NEED TO FIX THIS!

DON'T WORRY, DANI. EVERYTHING'S GONNA BE OK NOW.

NOW THAT I'VE FOUND YOU.

I'VE BEEN LOOKING FOR YOU FOR SO LONG.

THIS PLACE IS SO COLD AND LONELY...

IS THIS HOW YOU FEEL, DANI?

HAVE YOU BEEN ON YOUR OWN, LOCKED UP IN HERE ALL THIS TIME?

DORIAN...

I'M SO SORRY...

I'M GLAD YOU'RE HERE.

YOU'LL STAY WITH ME NOW. AND I WON'T BE ALONE ANYMORE!

HUH?

STAY?

BUT I DIDN'T COME TO STAY.
ARE...
ARE YOU GONNA LEAVE AGAIN?
NO!
I MEAN... YES, BUT YOU'RE COMING WITH ME, DANI.
WHERE?
WHAT DO YOU MEAN, WHERE?
WELL... AH...
WHERE?
THINK, DORIAN...
HOW DID I GET HERE?
HOW COULD I FORGET?
WHAT WAS I DOING BEFORE?
I NEED TO TAKE DANI WITH ME AS SOON AS POSSIBLE.
BUT I BELIEVE... I BELIEVE I'VE BEEN HERE BEFORE...
DORIAN... ARE YOU ALL RIGHT?
WHERE AM I?
THOSE PEOPLE EARLIER WEREN'T DAD OR MUM... SOMEONE'S TRYING TO FOOL ME. WHAT FOR?
...
HEY, TELL ME...
YOU'RE NOT REAL EITHER, ARE YOU?

NOTHING IS. DANI'S NOT HERE. YOU TOOK MY BIGGEST WISH TO USE IT AGAINST ME!
I THOUGHT YOUR FIRST ATTEMPTS TO SCARE ME OFF WERE CLUMSY,
BUT YOU WERE ONLY TRYING TO FOOL ME INTO THINKING THAT YOU DIDN'T WANT ME TO SEE DANI!
DANI HAS NEVER BEEN HERE IN THE FIRST PLACE!
WHAT ARE YOU SAYING, DORIAN?
IT'S REALLY ME. I'M DANI!
WHO ELSE COULD I BE?
WHO?
THE CAT!
AH!

WRETCHED...

KID...!

AAAAAH!

LET ME GO!

ARGH...

UGH...

GET OUT OF ME!

IT'S TRYING TO POSSESS ME!
AH!
THE WAND!
I HAVE TO...!
UGH...
DORIAN...?
GOOD...
YOUR EYES...!
NO...! DON'T TELL ME THAT YOU ARE...?
NO.
I'M OKAY.

CHAPTER 71

THE CAT...

IT'S NOT THE CAT ANYMORE...

I CAN DO THIS.

IT'S...

IT'S TOO EASY.

IN REALITY, THIS SPIRIT IS SO WEAK.

THE SPIRIT IS THERE!

COULD IT BE...?

YES... THE POWER CAME FROM DANI ALL LONG.

BUT THEN...

WHAT HAPPENED TO YOU?

YOU'RE WAY MORE POWERFUL THAN I AM.

LET ME GO!
NO!
I WON'T LET YOU GET AWAY!!
YOU ARE STRONGER, DANI.
BRAVER.
YOU STILL HAVEN'T FIGURED IT OUT, YOU IDIOT?
I WAS JUST PASSING BY!
BUT THEN, HOW COULD IT POSESS YOU?

I SAW A GOLDEN OPPORTUNITY TO HAVE A GOOD FEAST.

GETTING RID OF ME WON'T HELP YOU, THOUGH.

THERE'S SOMETHING WAY MORE POWERFUL...

YOUR SISTER ISN'T COMING BACK.

YOU LEARNED HOW TO DO THAT BY READING THOSE CREEPY NOTES?

DORIAN, DUDE, THAT WAS IMPRESSIVE!

WHOA...

WHAT...? WHAT HAPPENED?

I THINK WE FELL ASLEEP.

I JUST HAD THE WEIRDEST DREAM...

MY CUPCAKES WERE BURNING THE ENTIRE TIME.

I DREAMT OF CANNIBAL MERMAIDS...

AND AMIR WAS THERE TOO, LAZING AROUND THE ENTIRE TIME. HOW WEIRD.

IT WAS THAT DEMON; IT WAS TRYING TO DRIVE US CRAZY WITH TERROR!

I HAD A TERRIBLE TIME!

SO IT WAS THE SPIRIT PLAYING TRICKS...!

IT WAS ALSO POSSESSING YOU... ISN'T THAT RIGHT, MININO?

MEOW!

I CAN'T BELIEVE IT'S FINALLY OVER!

DORIAN...

HUH?

ARE YOU ALL RIGHT?

DIDN'T YOU LISTEN TO WHAT THE SPIRIT SAID...?

?

AH! DANI! SHE'S AWAKE!

DANI...?

DANI...?

UH...

WHAT DO I LOOK LIKE?

SUPER HANDSOME.

COOL!

DANI... ARE YOU OK?

HOW ARE YOU FEELING? CAN YOU REMEMBER ME?

...

... NO.

WHAT ABOUT ME? REMEMBER ME?

YES, NICO.

CAN YOU REMEMBER HOW WE MET?

... YOU WERE...IN THE DARK CASTLE.

...

WHAT ABOUT EVERYONE ELSE? CAN YOU REMEMBER ALL THESE PEOPLE?

... NO.

DAMIEN... WHAT'S GOING ON? WHY DIDN'T IT WORK?

I DON'T KNOW.

DORIAN SUPPOSEDLY GOT RID OF THE EVIL SPIRIT THAT WAS POSSESSING HER, BUT...

DANI... TELL ME, WOULD YOU LIKE TO COME TO THE SHELTER WITH US?

ALL RIGHT.

GOOD...

COME ON, STAND UP!

IF IT'S HARD FOR YOU TO WALK, I'LL CARRY YOU!

YOU KNOW I CAN HANDLE YOUR WEIGHT. I'M STRONG NOW.

I CAN WALK.

OKAY... IT SEEMS LIKE SHE IS NO LONGER AGGRESSIVE NOW THAT THE SPIRIT IS GONE...

LET'S TAKE HER TO THE SHELTER.

WE ALL NEED SOME SLEEP. AND A GOOD SHOWER! I'M PRETTY SURE WE STINK.

WE'LL TAKE CARE OF DANI THERE. COME ON!

UGH...

AH... DORIAN?

I...I'M SORRY!

I CAN'T... UGH...

HEY...

!

DORIAN, WAIT!

WHERE ARE YOU GOING?!

HEY, MONICA!
I'M GONNA TALK TO HIM! GET GOING, WE'LL JOIN YOU LATER!
WILL THEY BE OK?
YES... THE MOST DANGEROUS THING THEY CAN COME ACROSS IN THESE MOUNTAINS IS A WILD BOAR...
WAIT!
DORIAN, PLEASE STOP!
SINCE WHEN CAN YOU RUN SO FAST?!
PLEASE...!
DORIAN...!
AH...

UUUGH...

UGH...

DORIAN...

HEY...

SHE DOESN'T REMEMBER, MONICA! SHE DOESN'T REMEMBER ME!

I THOUGHT I COULD SAVE HER...

BUT I COULDN'T DO ANYTHING.

OF COURSE YOU DID! SHE'S WITH US NOW.

SHE'S NOT! THAT'S NOT DANI!

SHE'S SAFE!

WE CAN BRING HER BACK, DORIAN. WE'LL HEAL HER. ALL OF US.

WE'LL FIGURE OUT WHAT HAPPENED AND FIND A SOLUTION.

YOU DON'T GET IT, MONICA...

THE SPIRIT... BEFORE IT DISAPPEARED, IT TOLD ME...

IT TOLD ME DANI WASN'T COMING BACK, THAT SOMETHING POWERFUL WAS HOLDING HER BACK...

AND ARE YOU GONNA TRUST AN EVIL SPIRIT?

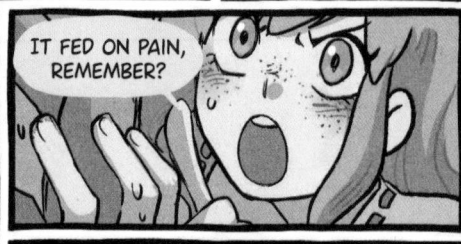

IT FED ON PAIN, REMEMBER?

IT JUST WANTED TO HURT YOU.

...

UH... BUT HOW'S IT POSSIBLE... THAT SHE DOESN'T REMEMBER ME?

MONICA...

I'M TIRED.

YES...

TONIGHT... DAMN, IT WAS SCARY.

AND YOU DIDN'T SEE THE GIANT SNAKE!

I PROMISE WE'LL FIND A SOLUTION.

TOGETHER.

UH...

THANK YOU...

FOR EVERYTHING.

SERIOUSLY, I...

AH...

I...

UH...

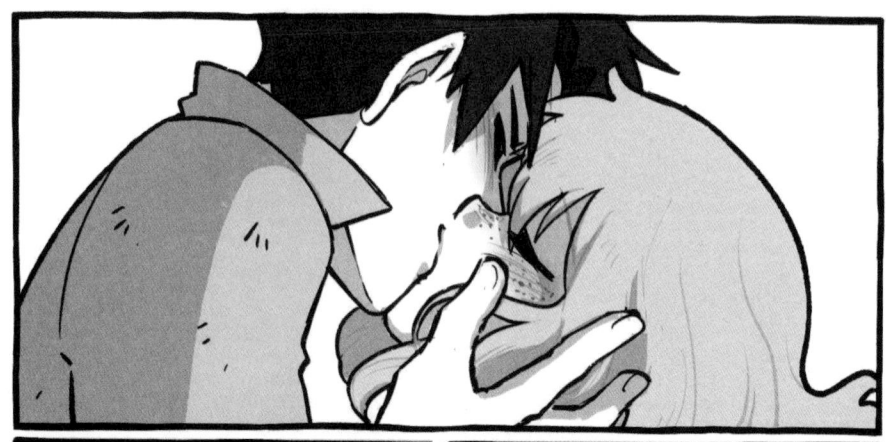

ARE YOU FEELING BETTER?

YES.

DO YOU WANT TO JOIN THE OTHERS?

NO.

CHAPTER 72

TOC
TOC
TOC
HEY, AISHA!
SUCH GOOD WEATHER TODAY! IT DOESN'T LOOK LIKE IT RAINED ALL NIGHT!
DO YOU NEED HELP?
WELL, YES! BRING ME SOME MORE WOODEN BOARDS, PLEASE.
OKAY. I'LL BE RIGHT BACK.
IT'S SO NICE OF YOU TO COME BACK TO REPAIR OUR HOME...
DON'T MENTION IT, MADAM!
THE DESTRUCTION OF THE SHELTER WAS OUR FAULT AFTER ALL.

WELL, IT'S NOT REALLY YOUR FAULT...

IT WAS ACTUALLY THE WITCH WHO DID IT...

EVEN THOUGH SHE DOESN'T LOOK DANGEROUS NOW.

JUST A BIT STUNNED.

IS SHE OK?

YES, MADAM, SHE'S STILL IN SHOCK.

WHY DID YOU BRING HER HERE?

SHE'S GONNA EAT US ALL!

DANI ISN'T GONNA HURT ANYONE.

WE'VE SAID IT BEFORE, SHE WAS POSSESSED BY AN EVIL SPIRIT.

HOW CAN YOU BE SO SURE, THOUGH? HOW DID YOU GET RID OF THE SPIRIT?

WHAT?

USING MAGIC, OF COURSE!

THAT'S WHAT MAGIC IS FOR!

MARK, CAN I HELP YOU WITH ANYTHING?
DO YOU HAVE YOUR WAND, DAMIEN?
NO... I THINK DORIAN MUST HAVE KEPT IT.
I CAN WORK WITH MY HANDS, THOUGH.
HMMM... DO YOU KNOW HOW TO MAKE CONCRETE?
NO.
ALL RIGHT, I'LL SHOW YOU.
PLEASE, SHOW ME...
I'M BEGGING YOU...
HOW CAN I HELP DANI?
HOW CAN I BRING HER BACK TO THE PERSON SHE WAS BEFORE?
AAARGH!
THE SAME IMAGE ONCE AGAIN!
STUPID CRYSTAL BALL! I'VE ALREADY SEEN THAT!

THERE'S NOTHING IN THAT IMAGE APART FROM DANI, AND THAT WRETCHED CAT AND I!

AND THE CAT ISN'T A PROBLEM ANYMORE...

I'M OVERLOOKING SOMETHING HERE.

BUT WHAT?

DANI...

I'D BETTER DISCUSS THIS WITH THE OTHERS. MAYBE TOGETHER WE'LL DISCOVER SOMETHING...

AH...

IT'S WEIRD TO FINALLY HAVE HER HERE.

NOT FOR ME. I'VE LIVED LIKE THIS FOR THREE YEARS.

TO BE HONEST, IT FEELS LIKE WE'RE BACK TO THE STARTING POINT.

THAT SPIRIT ATTACHED ITSELF TO HER LIKE A TICK, TAKING ADVANTAGE OF HER WEAKNESS TO DOMINATE HER.

BUT WHAT MADE HER WEAK IN THE FIRST PLACE?

HERE, YOUNG LADY...

CAREFUL NOT TO CATCH A COLD.

YOU SHOULD GO INSIDE. I'M GOING TO GET BREAKFAST READY, IT'S GETTING LATE.

NOW THAT SHE MENTIONS IT...

IT'S CERTAINLY GETTING LATE.

WHERE ARE THOSE TWO?

UH... WHAT TIME IS IT...?

DID I FALL ASLEEP...?

AH, DORIAN!

OH MY, OH MY.

WAAAAAA!

MONICA, I HAD A GREAT IDEA!

I KNOW HOW TO MAKE DANI REMEMBER ME.

I'VE GOT A BRILLIANT PLAN.

A PLAN?

YES! COME ON, STAND UP! WE NEED TO EXPLAIN MY PLAN TO EVERYONE!

COMING!

HEY, YOU, GUARD! GET ME OUT OF HERE.
IMPOSSIBLE, MRS. HILDE. YOUR POWERS CONSTITUTE A PUBLIC DANGER.
THAT'S NONSENSE!
MY SISTER-IN-LAW WAS A DANGER, AND YOU JUST TOOK AWAY HER MAGIC AND LET HER GO FREE.
I DEMAND YOU TAKE AWAY MY MAGIC TOO!
I WANT TO SPEAK TO QUEEN MONICA.
A WITCH WILLING TO GIVE UP HER POWERS?
I DON'T CARE. I'M RICH.
MONEY IS THE GREATEST POWER OF ALL.
TELL THEM I DON'T WANT MY POWERS EITHER.
ARE YOU ALSO RICH?
NO. I DON'T HAVE ANYTHING, NOT ANYMORE...
THESE POWERS ARE A BURDEN, THOUGH. A CURSE.
I DON'T WANT TO SEE THE FUTURE EVER AGAIN.

STOP COMPLAINING, AMIR. YOU HAVEN'T DONE ANYTHING USEFUL UNTIL NOW!

YOU'RE THE FEARLESS ONE, AISHA!

I'M NOT GOOD AT ANYTHING THAT IMPLIES MOVING FROM THE DIVAN, YOU KNOW THAT.

I GET THIS FROM MOTHER.

I CAN HEAR YOU.

SHUT UP AND COME. YOU'RE SO LAZY!

AISHA, YOU'VE JUST COME BACK AND YOU'RE LEAVING AGAIN?

MONICA NEEDS US!

TURNS OUT WE'LL BE SAVING THE DAY IN THE END.

DORIAN HAS A PLAN!

WE'LL GIVE DANI HER MEMORY BACK, AND WE NEED PEOPLE WHO KNEW HER THREE YEARS AGO!

SO COME ON, THERE'S NO TIME TO LOSE!

CHAPTER 73

DID YOU BRING HER CLOTHES?

HELLO, PRINCESS MONICA! OH...YOUR MAJESTY, NOW? IT'S BEEN SO LONG!

HI, MR. EVANS! IS EVERYTHING ALL RIGHT?

YES, SHE'S TAKING A BATH.

YES... BUT LOOK AT THIS!

THIS IS UNACCEPTABLE!

THAT'S WHAT SHE WAS WEARING EARLIER, ISN'T IT?

YES! CAN YOU BELIEVE IT?!

DORIAN PERFORMED ONE OF THOSE SPELLS TO FIX THE DAMAGE, AND THAT'S IT!

I TOLD HIM DANI COULDN'T JUST GO AROUND DRESSED AS AN EVIL WITCH! NO WAY!

I EVEN OFFERED TO GO SHOPPING MYSELF!

SHOPPING...? IT SEEMS DIFFICULT, JUDGING BY THE STATE OF THE VILLAGE...

ALL BUSINESSES CLOSED WHEN THE WAR BROKE OUT.

THOUGH THERE IS A LADY WHO USED TO BE A DRESSMAKER...

THAT SOUNDS PERFECT!

ARE YOU GONNA DESIGN IT? CAN YOU DRAW?

NO, BUT I'M A VERY CREATIVE PERSON.
IT'S JUST THAT... I DON'T THINK MY CLOTHES WOULD FIT HER.
WHY DON'T YOU JUST LEND HER SOMETHING?
...
I BET YOU'RE CARRYING A WHOLE CLOSET IN YOUR SUITCASE.
SHE'S... VERY TALL.
WE'VE GOT A LOT OF WORK TO DO!
NICO, WAIT!
HERE ARE YOUR CLOTHES!
?
NICO, YOU'VE RUINED ALL THE FUN!
YOU WERE GETTING ON MY NERVES!
WE HAVE MORE IMPORTANT THINGS TO DO!
NOW THAT YOU MENTION IT, DORIAN TOLD ME HE NEEDED YOUR HELP FOR THE PLANS.
LET'S GO!
DRINK THIS, DONATO.
YOU'LL FEEL BETTER SOON, DON'T WORRY.
HEY, DORIAN!

TALKING TO YOURSELF AGAIN?

I'M TALKING TO DONATO.

MONICA SAYS THAT YOU NEED MY INVALUABLE HELP.

OF COURSE! I'M THE KEY TO SOLVING THE MYSTERY WHICH HOLDS DANI CAPTIVE.

THANK YOU FOR FINDING NICO, DESPITE HOW STUBBORN I GOT OVER DANI'S CLOTHES.

...

HEY, ARE YOU LISTENING?

OH, YEAH, I'M SORRY.

THAT'S RIGHT, I NEED YOUR HELP.

WHAT DO WE NEED TO DO, THEN?

WE NEED TO REBUILD MASTER PENDRAGON'S HOUSE, JUST AS IT WAS BEFORE THE FLAMES DESTROYED IT.

WE NEED TO BE PRECISE, CAREFUL THAT EACH DETAIL IS EXACTLY LIKE OLD TIMES.

THAT'S WHY I NEED TO MAKE A REBUILDING PLAN BETWEEN US THREE.

YOU LIVED HERE LONGER THAN ANYONE ELSE, NICO, SO I TRUST YOUR MEMORY.

CONSIDER IT DONE.

KING WILLIAM WENT LOOKING FOR BRICKS, STONE, WOOD...

MATERIALS THAT WE NEED TO RECONSTRUCT THE HOUSE.

IN THE MEANTIME, I SENT DAMIEN TO LOOK FOR A WAND, SINCE MINE BROKE.
I TOLD HIM TO BORROW IT FROM A NEIGHBOR.
MANY WITCHES LIVE IN THE AREA NOW; MAYBE SOMEONE WILL HELP US.
WHEN I WOKE UP AFTER THREE YEARS, I FELT VERY STRANGE.
EVERYTHING WAS DIFFERENT; WE HAD ALL GROWN UP ALL OF A SUDDEN.
PERHAPS THE SAME HAPPENED TO DANI.
MAYBE SHE DIDN'T RECOGNIZE ME 'CAUSE I'VE CHANGED TOO MUCH.
MAYBE IF WE MANAGE TO MAKE THIS WORLD RESEMBLE THE ONE SHE LOVED AND LEFT BEHIND...
MAYBE AT THAT POINT...
SHE'LL BE ABLE TO REMEMBER AND COME BACK.
SO, THE LAST PART OF THE PLAN, THE MOST IMPORTANT...
LEAVE IT TO ME, OF COURSE!

YAY! I'M SO HAPPY!

I WILL DO MY BEST!

I CAN'T BELIEVE WHAT I'M ABOUT TO SAY, BUT...

FOR ONCE, I TRUST THIS SILLY PLAN OF YOURS!

I'M SURE IT'LL WORK!

COME ON, LET'S GET TO WORK!

SOOTHSAYER
WHOAAAA, IMPRESSIVE.
IT'S BACK TO HOW IT WAS BEFORE THE FIRE!
PERFECT.
IT'S ALMOST READY...

DINNER'S ALMOST READY!
WHAT ABOUT THESE SPIDER WEBS?
WE'VE ONLY BUILT THE HOUSE TODAY!
IT NEEDED TO LOOK AS REALISTIC AS POSSIBLE.
THAT'S INCREDIBLE, THE HOUSE TURNED OUT PERFECTLY!
IDENTICAL!
MAKES ME CRY!
YOU USED TO LIVE AMONG MICE AND SPIDER WEBS, MONICA? YOU?!
I CAN'T BELIEVE IT.
I'VE TOUGHENED UP, AFTER ALL!
WE CLEARLY NEED TO CELEBRATE TODAY'S ACCOMPLISHMENTS.
LET'S PARTY!
DON'T BE SILLY, WILL.
WE HAVE AN IMPORTANT MISSION TO ACCOMPLISH TOMORROW.
WE NEED TO GO TO BED EARLY AND REST!

SINCE WHEN DID YOU BECOME SO BORING, MONICA?
YOU'VE ALWAYS BEEN MY SIDEKICK AT ALL THE PALACE PARTIES!
HA HA HA
SHUT UP, WILL!
I REMEMBER THAT TIME YOU GOT SO EXCITED YOU ENDED UP DANCING ON TOP OF THE TABLE!
WILLIAM!
HOW CUTE!
MAKE SOME SPACE--HURRY UP, THE DISHES ARE HOT.
FINALLY! I'M SO HUNGRY.
...
ACTUALLY, NICO IS RIGHT.
IT'S INCREDIBLE TO BE HERE AGAIN.
MY PARENTS' MANSION AND THIS HOUSE ARE THE ONLY PLACES I CALL HOME,
AND THEY ENDED UP BEING DESTROYED BY FLAMES.
BOTH TIMES I FELT LIKE I WAS ADRIFT, WITH NO PLACE TO COME BACK TO.
IT WAS DEVASTATING...
AND DESPITE THAT, I'M HERE NOW...
... AT HOME.

...
I'M SO SORRY, DORIAN.
TO BE HONEST, I NEVER CONSIDERED OUR PARENTS' HOUSE MY HOME.
I RAN AWAY AS SOON AS I COULD,
AND I FOUND MY HOME WITH WILLIAM AND MONICA.
I DIDN'T THINK...
I SHOULDN'T HAVE LEFT YOU... UH...
WELL...
NEVER MIND.
THIS PLACE HAS ALWAYS BEEN MY ONLY HOME.
BUT...
FINDING OUT THAT THE MAN YOU CONSIDER A FATHER IS A HORRIBLE PERSON,
CAPABLE OF KILLING KIDS BY POISONING THEM...
I DON'T KNOW...
I FEEL LIKE I NEED TO SOMEHOW APOLOGIZE ON HIS BEHALF.
SINCE I FOUND OUT WHAT THE MASTER DID, DORIAN, I...
WHAT HE DID SPOILED ALL THE FOND MEMORIES I HAD OF HIM IN THIS HOUSE.
I LOVE HIM, BUT HE'S A DESPICABLE PERSON.
I'M SO SORRY...
FORGIVE ME, DORIAN...

CHAPTER 74

HEY, NICO... LISTEN...

THANK YOU FOR SAYING THAT.

BUT YOU SHOULD STOP TORTURING YOURSELF.

I STILL LOVE MY PARENTS. I WANT MY MUM TO REDEEM HERSELF AND REBOOT HER LIFE,

DESPITE THE FACT THAT THEY STARTED A GRUESOME WAR AND TRIED TO INVOLVE THEIR OWN CHILDREN.

AND THEY KILLED MY PARENTS.

THAT'S RIGHT, THEY KILLED MONICA'S PARENTS.

THEY ALSO KILLED MANY NEIGHBORS IN THE VILLAGE, SOME OF MY FRIENDS' MOTHERS AND FATHERS, WHEN I WAS A LITTLE BOY.

IT WAS TRAUMATIZING.

AND BEFORE THAT, MY FATHER ORDERED YOUR MOTHER TO BE BURNED FOR SIMPLY BEING A WITCH.

I SUPPOSE HE'S TO BLAME FOR ALL OF THIS.

WELL, IN TRUTH, THE FIRST ONE WHO SENT HUNDREDS OF WITCHES TO THE STAKE WAS MY FATHER.

HE'S ALSO TO BE BLAMED...

OKAY, I GET IT.
YOU'VE GOT A POINT THERE.
EVERY ADULT IN OUR LIVES WAS AWFUL.
THAT'S FOR SURE.
AND THAT'S BECAUSE THEY WERE SCARED OF ONE ANOTHER.
WE NEED TO BE BETTER THAN THAT.
WE'LL ALWAYS BE BETTER, I'M SURE OF IT.
MARK'S DAD IS A COOL DUDE, THAT'S FOR SURE!
THAT'S TRUE!
THAT'S OBVIOUSLY WHY YOU'RE SO COOL, TOO!
AH... NICO, I...
RIGHT! ENOUGH SENTIMENTALITY FOR TODAY.
LET'S EAT. IT'S GETTING COLD!
YOU'RE ALSO COOL, NICO...
RIGHT, RIGHT! LEAVE ME ALONE!

YOU CAN SLEEP IN THAT ROOM, DAMIEN.
THAT'S WHERE DANI USED TO SLEEP.
IN CASE YOU NEED ANYTHING, I'LL BE IN THE LOFT, JUST UP THE TRAP DOOR.
THANKS.
I...
... GOODNIGHT.
DAMIEN... HELP ME...
WHY ARE YOU CRAWLING ON THE FLOOR?
CAN WE TALK?
I NEED A FRIENDLY SHOULDER TO CRY ON.
SURE, BUT LET GO OF MY LEG.
DAMIEN, THIS IS TERRIBLE.
WHAT?
MONICA TOLD ME THAT...
THAT SHE AND DORIAN ARE DATING.

WHAT?
WHAT IS MONICA DOING WITH MY LITTLE BROTHER?
WAAAIT!
DON'T LEAVE ME ALONE...
IT'S JUST THAT I... UGH...
HOW CAN MONICA PLAY WITH ME LIKE THAT?
SERIOUSLY...? LOOK WHO'S TALKING...
BUT... PERHAPS...?
HAVE YOU REALIZED YOU'RE IN LOVE WITH HER AND YOU WANNA FIGHT FOR HER LOVE?
NO WAY! IT'S NOT THAT!
BUT I THOUGHT THAT ONCE WE WERE MARRIED, WE'D BEHAVE LIKE HUSBAND AND WIFE.

ALL MY LIFE I'VE BEEN PREPARING TO BE THE PERFECT KING.

BUT NOW MONICA SUGGESTS THAT WE CAN BE GOOD MONARCHS AND DO WHATEVER WE WANT WITH OUR LIVES.

YEAH, I KNOW THE DRILL.

YOU DON'T KNOW WHAT TO DO WITH YOUR LIFE.

EXACTLY!

I MAY JUST HAVE TO DO THE SAME THING SHE DOES!

WHAT...?

THE SAME THING?

YEP!

SMOOCHING WITH A WITCH BOY!

HEY...

WHY AREN'T YOU PUSHING ME AWAY LIKE YOU USUALLY DO?

WHY SHOULD I?
YOU AND MONICA ARE NOT IN LOVE.
IT WOULDN'T HURT ANYONE.
YOU ALREADY KNOW WHAT I WANT, WILL.
IT'S UP TO YOU NOW.
IF YOU MEAN IT, THEN I...
UH, I...
SORRY.
YOU'RE LEAVING?
YOU WON'T EVEN WISH ME GOODNIGHT?
GOOD NIGHT, DAMIEN.
SLAM

...
BUT THAT WAS NICE.
KNOCK KNOCK KNOCK
WILL...?
AH.
... HI.
WHY DO YOU LOOK SLIGHTLY DISAPPOINTED?
UM, WELL...
TELL ME, DO YOU NEED ANYTHING?
WELL, I... COULDN'T SLEEP, AND...
I WANTED TO THANK YOU.
EH?
YES... YOU'VE HELPED US A LOT.
I'M SORRY I DIDN'T TRUST YOU IN THE BEGINNING.

MUM AND DAD SET ME AGAINST YOU. IT WAS ALL VERY CONFUSING AND...

NOW I DO SEE YOU'RE A GOOD PERSON, DAMIEN.

AND I'M NOT SCARED OF YOU ANYMORE.

YOU'RE THE ONLY OLDER BROTHER I'VE GOT, AND...

I'D LIKE FOR US TO REALLY BEHAVE LIKE BROTHERS FROM NOW ON.

DORIAN...

I'M SO SORRY I ABANDONED BOTH YOU AND DANI IN THAT HOUSE.

HUH?

I LEFT KNOWING THAT IT WAS A TOXIC PLACE. I LEFT YOU BEHIND.

I WAS A SCARED KID, AND...

AND I'M SELFISH. THAT'S THE TRUTH.

I'VE NEVER BEEN ABLE TO FORGIVE MYSELF.

I THOUGHT I WOULDN'T NEED TO FACE IT. I TRIED TO GET YOU OUT OF MY HEAD, PRETEND YOU DIDN'T EXIST.

BUT YOU'RE HERE NOW, SAYING THAT YOU WANNA FIX THINGS.

INCLUDING OUR FAMILY.

OF COURSE. IT'S ALL GETTING FIXED.

...

WHAT HAPPENED DOESN'T MATTER, DAMIEN.
REALLY.
WHEN ALL OF THIS IS OVER,
I'LL GO LIVE WITH DANI AND MAYBE WITH MUM, IF THAT'S POSSIBLE.
YOU CAN ALSO LIVE WITH US, IF YOU WISH.
MAYBE YOU COULD HAVE A HOME THIS TIME AROUND.

SHE LOOKS QUITE HARMLESS WHEN SHE'S ASLEEP.

AISHA! WHEN DID YOU ARRIVE?

A FEW HOURS AGO.

THE OTHERS ARE DOWNSTAIRS, EMPTYING YOUR FATHER'S CUPBOARD.

ARE... ARE YOU SURE WE'RE ALLOWED TO EAT ALL THESE CAKES?

IF ANYONE ASKS YOU, JUST SAY YOU HAVEN'T SEEN ANYTHING.

WE'VE BEEN HAVING DINNER AT THE MASTER'S HOUSE. YOU SHOULD HAVE COME, AISHA!

YEAH, YOUR FATHER TOLD ME...

I DON'T KNOW. I DIDN'T WANT TO BOTHER YOU BY JOINING THE GROUP WITHOUT WARNING...

BOTHER?
PFFF.
YEAH, WELL...
DO YOU THINK IT WILL WORK?
WHAT ARE YOU TALKING ABOUT? YOU'RE PART OF THE GROUP!
I MEAN, THE PLAN.
DO YOU THINK DANI WILL REGAIN HER MEMORY?
HMM...
YES.
I HAVE A FEELING...
...THAT EVERYTHING WILL BE OKAY.

CHAPTER 75

DORIAN...

ARE YOU READY?

Y... YES... AND YOU?

YES!

WHOAAAAAA!

YOU'RE...

YOU'RE...

DON'T LAUGH.

WHY WOULD I LAUGH?!

I WAS RIGHT!

YOU LOOK SO COOL IN SHORTS!

SUCH LOVELY LEGS!

YEAH, ALL RIGHT MONICA... I'M EMBARRASSED...

AH...

SO CUUUTE!

HEY!

YOU WERE WEARING THOSE SHORTS THE FIRST TIME I SAW YOU. REMEMBER?

I USED TO CALL YOU FROG-KID!

YES... AND I TRIED TO IMPRESS YOU... HOW PATHETIC.

OH, BUT YOU IMPRESSED AND ALSO SCARED ME.

AAAAAH! WHAT ARE YOU TALKING ABOUT!

YOU'RE NOT CUTE ANYMORE!

I NOTICED I EARNED YOUR ADMIRATION WHEN YOU STOPPED CALLING ME FROG-KID,

AND YOU STARTED CALLING ME PROFESSOR WYTTE.

HEY, YOU TWO!

264

ARE YOU ALREADY FIGHTING, FIRST THING IN THE MORNING?
HELLO.
NICOOOO!
SO MANY MEMORIES. I'M GONNA CRY!
WHAT I DON'T GET IS WHY I'M DRESSED AS MASTER PENDRAGON.
DANI DOESN'T KNOW YOU, AND WE CAN'T BRING THE REAL PENDRAGON. YOU ARE THE PERFECT CANDIDATE.
AH!
DORIAN!
WHAT IS IT?
THOSE SHORTS! THEY'RE THE SAME ONES I SAW IN THE CRYSTAL BALL!
LOOKING AT THIS HORRIBLE IMAGE WILL BE WORTH IT! FOR DANI!
REALLY? THAT'S AWESOME!
ALTHOUGH THE OTHER VISION, WITH DANI CRYING IN FRONT OF THE PYRE?
I STILL DON'T UNDERSTAND THAT ONE...
DING DONG

DING DONG

SHE'S HERE!

COMING! WAIT A MINUTE!

DING DONG

MAKE SURE TO OPEN THE DOOR FROM THE FLOOR, MAJESTY!

YES!

AND CRYING! CRYING IS VERY IMPORTANT!

DING DONG

SEE YOU SOON!

DING DONG

GOOD LUCK!

DING DONG

OH, HI CARLO!

DO YOU KNOW YOUR LINES, BUDDY?

AH...

HELLO...

YOU'RE FINALLY HERE!

WELCOME!

...

COME ON IN, COME ON IN.

YOUR BROTHER'S WAITING FOR YOU INSIDE.

HERE, HAVE A SEAT, YOUNG LADY.

GREAT.

I'M GONNA MAKE YOU SOME HOT CHOCOLATE NOW, KIDS.

AHEM...

WHAT A MESS, HUH DANI?

IT WAS SUCH BAD LUCK, MISSING OUR SCHOOL BUS LIKE THAT!

WE'RE HOPELESS!

... BUS?

THERE YOU GO, KIDS.

THANKS.

UH...

PRINCE WILLIAM, REMEMBER YOUR LINE: "I ACCEPT YOU BOTH AS..."

OH, RIGHT!

CHILDREN, I ACCEPT YOU BOTH AS APPRENTICES...

TO FIGHT AGAINST THE EVIL WITCHES!

COOL!

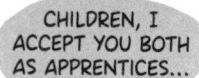

SLURP

...

DING DONG

OPEN THE DOOR, MASTER!

PRINCESS MONICA'S HERE TO TALK TO YOU!

WELCOME, MY DEAR PRINCESS MONICA!

HI THERE!

AH... HELLO...

LET ME INTRODUCE MYSELF.

I'M DORIAN, HEIR OF THE WYTTE FAMILY.

AH... WHAT A CUTE KID!

...

HI DANI!

HELLO, NICO.

WHAT'S GOING ON?

SINCE PRINCESS MONICA'S HERE, WE'LL NEED TO BE CAREFUL NOT TO DO MAGIC!

SHE HATES WITCHES!

WHOOSH

EH...
AAAAH!
HELP!
THEY'RE EVIL WITCHES!
NO, WE'RE NOT EVIL!
GUARDS!
DON'T YOU WORRY, PRINCESS MONICA!
WE'LL DEFEND YOU!
I DON'T LIKE YOU, WEIRDO!
DON'T TOUCH ME!
HI EVERYONE. I BROUGHT CAKE.

EH. EASY THERE!
YOU'RE STILL STUDENTS!
EXACTLY, GO STUDY!
?
WE NEED TO LEARN GOOD SPELLS!
UM... YES...
READ THE BOOK.
AND PRACTICE.
YES, THAT'S IT.
LOOK, DANI!
NOW I KNOW HOW TO MAKE ICE!
CAN YOU REMEMBER THIS SPELL?
DANI, LOOK AT MY TOY CASTLE!
IT'S JUST LIKE MY REAL HOME!

DANI. I'M GONNA KILL YOU.
CAN YOU REMEMBER THE LOVE POTION THAT WENT WRONG?
WELL, I HATE YOU NOW.
LOOK, THE LITTLE AIRPLANE YOU NEED TO STEAL FROM MARK!
IS IT WORKING?
SHUT UP, WILL! YOU'RE SUPPOSED TO BE ASLEEP.
HEY...
DOES THIS RING A BELL?
WHAT ABOUT THE BALL? CAN YOU REMEMBER?
YOU LOOKED SO CUTE! DRESSED IN BLUE!

DORIAN.

THIS IS NOT WORKING.

...

WAIT.

CAN YOU REMEMBER THIS ROOM?

I USED TO SLEEP HERE,

AND YOU USED TO COME HERE WHEN YOU COULDN'T SLEEP.

COME ON, DANI! LET'S GO UPSTAIRS!

THIS IS WHERE WE REHEARSE OUR DANCE STEPS!

LOOK AT THAT! DO YOU REMEMBER IT?

HEY, DANI.

WHAT?

ARE YOU UP FOR A RACE?

A RACE?

YES.

DON'T YOU ENJOY FLYING?

LET'S GO!

DON'T BE A COWARD, DANI!

WE'RE GONNA FLY ON A BROOM!

ALL RIGHT.

AWESOME! YOU'RE GOING DOWN!

YOU'LL SEE HOW QUICK I AM, DANI!

READY...
SET...
GO!
WHOAAAA!
WHAT WAS THAT?
NICO CAN'T FLY BY HIMSELF, SO I HAD TO HELP.
UGH!
BUT WHAT ABOUT DANI...?
DANI NEVER NEEDED ANYBODY'S HELP...
SHE'S IMPRESSIVE WHEN SHE'S ON HER BROOM.

SHE LOOKS LIKE SHE WAS BORN TO FLY.
DANI!
CAN YOU REMEMBER NOW?
HUH?
WHAT IT FEELS LIKE TO FLY!
IT'S SO FUN!
RIGHT?
!

SPLASH!

AAAH!

WHAT'S THAT?!

DANI!

A MONSTER!

HURRY UP, WE NEED A BROOM!

OKAY!

IT LOOKS JUST LIKE THE GIANT OCTOPUS THAT WE KILLED!
COULD IT BE HIS SON?
I DON'T KNOW, MAYBE.
AH...!
DANI!
QUICK, NICO, HELP DANI OUT!
THAT'S WHAT I'M TRYING TO DO!
I CAN'T SEE HER!

OH NO!

SHE'S GONNA DROWN!

NICO, GET HER OUT OF THERE!

ARGH!

I NEED TO DO SOMETHING!

CARLO!

THERE YOU GO, DAMIEN.

DORIAN, TAKE THE BROOM.

NO, I WON'T BE OF ANY HELP WITH THAT.

I ACTUALLY NEED IT.

THANKS, DAMIEN.

IF ONLY I KNEW HOW TO USE A BOW...

AT LEAST I COULD HELP A LITTLE.

THROW SOME ROCKS AT THE MONSTER.

AISHA...

AS FAR AS I'M CONCERNED,

YOU'D BE AS USEFUL AS I AM, RIGHT NOW.

I CAN'T SEE ANY WEAKNESSES...
ALL I CAN SEE RIGHT THERE IS TENTACLES.
AAARGH!
DANI...
WHERE IS SHE?
DON'T TELL ME...
OH MY...
IT'S HUGE...
...
BUT NO TRACE OF DANI.

YOU'LL BE SORRY, YOU FOUL BEAST.

UH...

MY SPELL DIDN'T EVEN SCRATCH IT.

THEN LET'S SEE...

...IF YOU CAN DODGE MY BARRIER!

AT LEAST THIS WAY YOU'LL STAY STILL.

WHAT?!

HOW IS THIS POSSIBLE?!

DAMIEN'S SPELLS AREN'T WORKING...

THIS LOOKS BAD...

OUT OF THE WAY!

!

WAIT, MONICA! WHAT ARE YOU GONNA DO?

YOU CAN'T CAST SPELLS!

WAIT!

UGH!

IT SEEMS THAT DAMIEN'S SPELLS AREN'T HURTING THE MONSTER AT ALL!

NEITHER ARE THE ARROWS.

PERHAPS IF I FREEZE THE WATER SURROUNDING IT, IT'LL BE PARALYZED.

NO!

WE SHOULD ONLY ATTACK THE BEAST.

WE DON'T KNOW IF DANI'S STILL IN THE WATER!

SPELLS AND ARROWS AREN'T WORKING.

I HAVE TO DO SOMETHING.

FOR ONCE...

I HAVE TO BE USEFUL.

WH... WHAT...

WILL, YOU IDIOT, WHAT ARE YOU DOING?!

DON'T BE STUPID!

WILL...?

DAMIEN CAN'T GET ANGRY AT ME.

IT IS MY DUTY AS A KING TO PROTECT THEM ALL.

EVEN IF IT'S THE FIRST AND LAST TIME.

I'LL KILL YOU...

FROM INSIDE.

GULP
WHAT?! DID THE MONSTER JUST...?!
WATCH OUT!
IT'S FALLING DOWN!
WILLIAM!
IS EVERYONE OKAY?
YEAH... EXCEPT THE MONSTER...
AND KING WILLIAM...
KING WILLIAM SAVED US!

OH NO...!

THERE'S SOMETHING STRANGE HERE.

WE ATTACKED THE CREATURE WITH SPELLS AND ARROWS... BUT THERE'S NOT A SINGLE SCRATCH.

DID IT REALLY DIE JUST FROM WILLIAM'S ATTACK?!

IS IT A SEA SNAKE?

WHOA, IT'S HUGE!

IT ATE THE KING!

AISHA! WHERE ARE YOU GOING?!

TO THE BATTLEFIELD!

WE'LL BE MORE USEFUL THERE!

GET OUT OF THE WAY, PLEASE!

LET ME THROUGH!

DON'T WORRY, WILL. I'M SURE I'VE GOT SOME POTION...

TO MAKE IT PUKE OR SOMETHING...?

MONICA GET AWAY FROM THERE!

IT'S DANGEROUS!

LET ME GO, DORIAN!

I NEED TO HELP WILL!

DORIAN'S RIGHT.

THIS IS REALLY ODD.

NICO...

DO YOU THINK IT HAS SWALLOWED DANI?

NO IDEA...

BUT LOOK AT ALL THAT SMOKE...

MAYBE THE MONSTER IS GOING TO EXPLODE.

WE MUST TAKE COVER NOW.

BUT WE NEED TO HELP WILL!

LEAVE THAT TO ME.

... DAMIEN?

I'M GONNA GET WILL OUT OF THERE.

I'LL OPEN THE SERPENT FROM TOP TO BOTTOM, IF NECESSARY.

AH... WAIT, NO...

THAT'S NOT SAFE EITH--

I'LL HELP YOU!

MONICA, THE SMOKE...!

EVERYBODY GET OUT OF THE WAY,

THINGS MIGHT GET DANGEROUS.

--DAMIEN, WAIT!

AH?!

WHY DID HE DO THAT? WHY DID WILL SACRIFICE HIMSELF WITH NO HESITATION...? IS HE DOING THAT BADLY? AM I THAT BLIND?

WELL, IT DOESN'T MATTER RIGHT NOW...

I'M COMING TO SAVE YOU, WILL.

DAMIEN!

LOOK...

WHAT THE...?

WATCH OUT, DAMIEN.

WHOAAAA!

HOW?!

WHERE DID YOU COME FROM?!

YOU ALMOST STUCK THE SWORD IN MY FOREHEAD.

WILL! YOU'RE FINE!

HE HE, YEAH, TURNS OUT THE MONSTER IS NOT A REAL ONE.

...

I WAS LUCKY ENOUGH TO FALL INTO THE WATER.

THAT WAS SCARY...!

I WAS IN A SEA MADE OF TENTACLES COVERING MY EYES,

ALTHOUGH I WASN'T ABLE TO TOUCH THEM.

I'M GLAD HE'S FINE...

BUT THIS IS REALLY CONFUSING.

DAMIEN!

ARE YOU CRYING?!

UH...

UGH...

COME HERE, GIVE ME A HUG!

I'LL COMFORT YOU!

NO WAY!

IT'S YOUR FAULT. YOU'RE SUCH AN IDIOT!

LOOK, IT'S TRUE!

THE MONSTER IS JUST A MIRAGE!

I CAN WALK THROUGH IT LIKE IT'S NOTHING!

BUT... WHO WOULD DO SUCH A THING?

AND...WHY?

THAT'S WHY IT HASN'T DESTROYED THE HOUSE OR ANYTHING ELSE!

...

...

DORIAN!

AH...!

DANI...!

THEY'VE USED THE MONSTER AS A DISTRACTION!

WITCHES, CLEARLY.

AND WE STUPIDLY FELL FOR IT.

WE MUST FIND HER, BEFORE THEY TAKE HER TOO FAR AWAY!

I WON'T LOSE DANI AGAIN!

I THINK SOMEONE TOOK HER!

I HOPE THE MONSTER HASN'T EATEN THEM.
HELP!
THAT VOICE...
MARK! OUR FRIENDS NEED US!
OVER THERE TOO!
SOMEONE'S IN DANGER!
BUT...!

CHAPTER 77

AH!

DANI!

THEY'RE TAKING HER AWAY!

PERHAPS THEY'RE TAKING HER TO SAVE HER FROM THE MONSTER.

HEY, MARK, OVER HERE!

BARRY!

WHERE'D YOU COME FROM?

THESE WITCHES ARE WELL-KNOWN FOLLOWERS OF ANGELA AND HANS...

THEY ATTEMPTED TO CANCEL OUR NEWSPAPER MULTIPLE TIMES.

WE TRIED TO STOP THEM, AND IF IT WASN'T FOR NOAH,

I'M PRETTY SURE THE WITCHES WOULD BE MILES AWAY BY NOW.

DANI!

DANI, COME BACK!

DON'T TRUST THOSE PEOPLE!

COME BACK TO US, COME ON!

LEAVE HER ALONE!

YOU'RE SUCH A DRAG.

MARK!

UGH!

ARE YOU OKAY?

YEAH... I'M FINE...

WE DON'T WANNA HURT YOU!

JUST LEAVE US ALONE.

LET US GO AND IT'LL ALL BE FINE.

BOOM

ARGH!

SARAH! ARE YOU ALL RIGHT?!

OH, COME ON!

WHO...?

IT'S
FUNNY.
'CAUSE IF YOU WON'T GIVE MY SISTER BACK...
I DO INTEND TO HURT YOU QUITE A BIT.
LISTEN, BOB, THAT GUY...
THAT GUY'S A WYTTE.
THE OLDER BROTHER IS ALSO THERE... AND THEY'VE GOT LOTS OF ARMED PEOPLE TOO.
KAT.
STOP IT.

THIS ISN'T THE TIME TO CHICKEN OUT.
DORIAN, WE MUST MAKE EVERYONE FALL OFF THEIR BROOMS.
IT'LL BE BETTER TO FIGHT THEM ON THE GROUND.
YES, YOU'RE RIGHT.
COME ON, DORIAN.
THIS ISN'T THE TIME FOR DISTRACTIONS.
I WON'T LET THEM TAKE YOU AWAY FROM ME AGAIN, DANI.
I WILL FIGHT.

WE WON'T LET YOU KIDNAP HER!

KIDNAP HER?

SHE'S MY SISTER!

SHE'S OUR QUEEN!

AISHA, WILLIAM, FOLLOW ME!

RIGHT NOW?!

THEY'VE ALREADY FALLEN OFF THEIR BROOMS, I CAN FINALLY HERD THEM AS WELL!

YES, RIGHT NOW!

...

AH!

DANI!

NICO, FOLLOW THEM!

GET RID OF THOSE TWO AND HIDE DANI IN A SAFE PLACE.

I'LL TAKE CARE OF THE REST.

SURE!

COME ON, NICO.

UGH...

I NEED TO SCARE THESE FOLKS AWAY.

WHY DID YOU HAVE TO SHOW UP RIGHT NOW?

WE WERE ALMOST THERE.

WE WERE SO CLOSE TO GETTING DANI BACK TO NORMAL.

AND YOU JUST HAD TO RUIN IT ALL.

DO... DORIAN IS...?

TEARING UP THE GROUND?

YOU'LL BE SORRY.

THIS CAN'T BE!

JULIA!

WAAAH, MUM, I DON'T LIKE THE NOISE!

HONEY, DON'T CRY.

THERE'S SO MUCH NOISE OUTSIIIDE!

DON'T BE AFRAID.

THE WITCHES WILL PROTECT US.

AH...

MARK, I'M ALSO AFRAID!

AISHA, WHAT ARE YOU LOOKING FOR?

ARROWS!

MONICA TOLD ME TO LOOK FOR ARROWS AND COVER THE TIPS WITH CLOTH.

AH!

THINGS ARE GETTING SERIOUS OUT THERE!

I'M GONNA GO OUT TO SEE IF I CAN HELP.

AHA!

HERE THEY ARE!

HE HE...

THEY ALL HAVE THEIR FEET ON THE GROUND.

NOW YOU'LL FIND OUT. YOU'LL SEE WHEN KING WILLIAM ENTERS THE SCENE...

THERE'S NO WAY.

YOU WON'T HURT ANYONE WITH THAT SWORD.

WHAT'S WITH THE HAT?

I'M NOT A WITCH LIKE YOU, MONICA...

THAT WE CAN BE GOOD MONARCHS.

WE WILL.

IT'S A SYMBOL.

IT MEANS THAT WE'RE NOT DIFFERENT FROM THEM.

NOT ANYMORE.

WE'LL FIGHT TO GET DANI BACK, BUT ALSO TO ACHIEVE PEACE.

IT MEANS THAT WE'RE NOT OUR FATHERS.

OH NO, THE ILLUSION DIDN'T KEEP THEM DISTRACTED LONG ENOUGH!
AND NOW, WITH NO BROOMS LEFT...
WHAT ARE WE GONNA DO?
SHOULD WE TAKE HER AWAY BE TRAIN?
BY BOAT?
WE NEED A CAR!
WE CAN'T ALLOW THEM TO LOCK THE QUEEN UP IN JAIL!
NOT SO FAST, YOU COWARDS!
POW
HEY!
TAKE YOUR FOOT OFF HIS FACE!
HUH?
MAKE ME.
AS YOU WISH, DUDE!
YOU SCREWED UP,
SAY GOODBYE TO YOUR...!
WHOA?!

IT'S A DRAGON FROG!

RUUUUN!

CRUSH THEM, CARLO!

A...

A FROG?

PHEW...

AND YOU, DANI... I WAS HOPING THE BROOM RACE HAD ACCOMPLISHED SOMETHING, BUT IT HASN'T...

LET'S GO!

ARE YOU OK?

LOOK, THE QUEEN IS RIGHT THERE!

WE NEED TO TAKE YOU TO A SAFE PLACE, DANI.

I THINK MY LEG'S HURT...

HAH! WHAT A BLOW!

NOT SO FAST!

CAREFUL, YOU IDIOT!

DON'T HURT THE QUEEN!

WHAT WERE YOU GONNA DO TO HER?

LOCK HER UP IN A DUNGEON, JUST LIKE MRS. WYTTE?

YOU'RE WRONG. DANI IS MY FRIEND.

THE QUEEN OF WITCHES WOULDN'T BE FRIENDS WITH SOMEONE LIKE YOU.

SOMEONE LIKE ME?

FOR YOUR INFORMATION, WE'RE THE SAME. I'M A WITCH TOO.

SHUT YOUR MOUTH, YOU PIECE OF TRASH!

COME ON THEN, IF YOU TRULY ARE A WITCH, PROVE IT!

CAST A SPELL. I'M WAITING!

I'M NOT THAT KIND OF WITCH...

HA-HA-HA-HA-HA!

RIGHT, DON'T MAKE ME LAUGH!

FIGHT ME.

I PROMISE I WON'T BE HARD ON YOU.

COME ON, I EVEN LENT YOU A WAND.

IF YOU'RE INCAPABLE OF DEFENDING YOURSELF, THOUGH...

I'LL KILL YOU.

COME ON NOW, IT'S NOT NECESSARY TO GO THAT FAR...
SHUT UP!
CAN'T YOU SEE WHAT THEY'RE TRYING TO DO?
BELITTLING OUR FIGHT, OUR STRUGGLE.
WE'RE NOT EQUALS.
WHAT DO YOU EVEN KNOW ABOUT MY STRUGGLES?
COME ON, DUDE.
FIGHT FOR YOUR LIFE.
I'LL RIP YOUR FACE OFF!
THAT'S CHEATING, SMARTYPANTS!
LET ME SEE YOUR AWESOME MAGICAL POWERS!
ON THE COUNT OF THREE...
ONE.
TWO.
THREE!

POW
CRASH
NICO!
ARE YOU...?!
AH!
WOW, YOU THREW A MEAN PUNCH THERE, MARK!
YOU COULD'VE WAITED FOR ME TO GET THE PARTY STARTED!
WHAT HAPPENED?!
IS DANI OK...?!
AH!

NICO! YOU'RE BLEEDING!
I'M... I'M FINE.
I KNEW BEING YOUR FRIEND WOULD PROVE TO BE USEFUL SOMEDAY, MARK.
AH... IDIOT...
COME, WE NEED TO TAKE CARE OF THAT WOUND.
WHAT'S WITH ALL THIS DARK SMOKE?
IT'S JUST LIKE THE SMOKE THAT SURROUNDS MY MOTHER...
SMOKE?
WHAT SMOKE?
OVER THERE. LOOK CLOSELY.
DON'T YOU WORRY, NICO. MONICA'S HERE TO SAVE YOU!
THIS'LL HELP STOP THE BLOOD FLOW! LET'S SPREAD IT ON YOUR...!
HUH?

DANI...
ARE YOU DOING THIS?
DAAAD!
I TOLD YOU TO HIDE. THIS IS DANGEROUS!
... DANI?
WHY ARE YOU DOING THIS TO US?
WHY CAN'T YOU LET US LIVE IN PEACE?
--NI!
WHAT THE...?!
WATCH OUT, MONICA!
WHAT'S THAT?!

... DANI!
CAN YOU HEAR ME?!
WHAT'S GOING ON?!
YOU'RE EVEN MORE ABSENT THAN USUAL.
DANI?
I'M FINE, NICO.
NO...
NOT AGAIN. YOUR FACE...
I REALLY HATE YOUR FACE.
I CAN'T STAND IT.
EVERY TIME I SEE THAT SORT OF EMOTIONLESS MASK,
I REMEMBER DANI.
THE REAL DANI.
THE ONE WHO SMILED AND GOT ANGRY AND LAUGHED AND CRIED.

YOU WERE ALWAYS SO EXPRESSIVE...

I REALLY LOVED THAT ABOUT YOU.

DANI, I...

I... I REALLY LOVED Y...

UGH...

BUT I DON'T KNOW WHAT TO DO ANYMORE TO MAKE THAT DANI COME BACK.

PLEASE, GIVE ME A HINT...

I'M BEGGING YOU.

I DON'T KNOW WHAT TO DO ANYMORE.

"LOOK CLOSELY."

312

"WHAT'S WITH ALL THE DARK SMOKE?"

HOW LONG HAS IT BEEN THERE?

WHAT...?

DENSE DARKNESS...

ALMOST PALPABLE.

WAIT, I...

I THINK IT HAS ALWAYS BEEN THERE...

JUST LIKE THE VISION IN THE CRYSTAL BALL.

BUT I STILL DON'T GET IT!
IF THERE WAS SMOKE ON THAT DAY, SO WHAT?!
WHO SURROUNDED YOU WITH ALL THAT DARKNESS?
COULD IT BE...?
COULD IT ALL BE MY FAULT, DANI?
THERE WAS NO ONE ELSE IN THAT VISION.
NICO...
JUST THAT DARN CAT, WHO IN THE END WAS NOTHING BUT AN OPPORTUNIST.
THERE'S ONLY ME LEFT. IT HAS TO BE ME!
HOW DO I FIX IT?
UGH...
IN THE VISION, IT'S ONLY ME AND...
AND...

OF COURSE.

WHAT...?

IT WASN'T ME...

THERE WAS SOMEONE ELSE THERE.

I'M SURE YOU DIDN'T EVEN KNOW WHAT YOU WERE DOING.

IT HAS ALWAYS BEEN YOUR SPECIALTY, DOING STUFF WITHOUT MEANING TO.

ALL THIS TIME...

IT WAS YOU ALL ALONG.

YOU...

YOU'VE CURSED YOURSELF, HAVEN'T YOU?

OH, DANI...

MY DANI...

HOW CLUMSY.

HURRY UP, WE NEED TO GET NICO OUT OF THERE!
YES...
ALTHOUGH IT'D BE GOOD FOR DANI TO STAY INSIDE AS WE SCARE THESE PEOPLE AWAY.
I CAN'T THINK OF A SAFER PLACE.
ALL RIGHT, I'M GONNA OPEN A HOLE IN THE STONE.
DON'T LET ANY WITCH GO NEAR THE STONE FORTRESS!

DON'T HURT ANYONE THOUGH!
WE CAN SOLVE THIS PEACEFULLY.
YOU SEEM VERY CONFIDENT...
TRUST ME, AISHA.
AWESOME!
BRUTAL.
HE GOT PETRIFIED. THAT'S A GOOD ONE.
IT WORKED!
IT'S JUST LIKE CASTING SPELLS.
WE MAKE A GOOD TEAM.
YES. I FEEL POWERFUL!
I COULD TEACH YOU HOW TO SHOOT AN ARROW IF YOU WANT.
THAT'D BE WONDERFUL...!
AH...
MONICA!
NO!

DON'T EVEN THINK ABOUT GETTING CLOSER, OR I'LL HURT YOUR QUEEN.
I... I CAN'T MOVE.
DO YOU THINK THIS IS FUNNY, HUH?
YOU ENJOY MESSING AROUND WITH POTIONS?
YOU THINK YOU'RE ONE OF US JUST BECAUSE YOU'RE WEARING THAT CUTE LITTLE HAT?
DON'T MAKE ME LAUGH.
YOU CAN'T FOOL ANYONE.
YOU'RE NOT A WITCH.
WHAT ABOUT THIS?
YOU'RE ONLY ABLE TO BREW POTIONS WHEN YOU FOLLOW A RECIPE.
YOU'RE NOTHING WITHOUT THIS.
CRASH
NICO'S POTION...!

RIGHT NOW, YOU'RE AT MY MERCY. I COULD KILL YOU IF I WANTED TO.
CAN YOU SEE THAT, LITTLE QUEEN?
BUT I'M NOT GONNA DO THAT.
'CAUSE I'M NOT LIKE YOU ALL.
AND NOW, SET OUR QUEEN FREE AND...
!!
LUCAS!
ARE YOU ALL RIGHT?
UGH...
Y... YEAH...
AAAARGH!
UGH!
COME ON.

CHAPTER 78

DISENCHANT THE QUEEN. NOW.

UNDO YOUR SPELL.

WAIT, DORIAN!

DON'T ATTACK HIM!

DORIAN, NO...!

NOT LIKE THIS!

I WON'T ASK TWICE.

ALL RIGHT!

ALL RIGHT, I'M LETTING HER GO!

AH...!

DORIAN...!
DORIAN, NO!
WHAT ARE YOU DOING?!
ARGH!
WELL, THEN.
YOU'RE GONNA GO NOW.
FAR AWAY.
AND YOU'RE GONNA LEAVE US ALONE. ALL OF YOU.
STOP IT NOW!
WE'RE NOT GONNA SOLVE ANYTHING LIKE THIS!

I'M SICK OF ALL THIS, MONICA!
YOU'RE GONNA KILL HIM, DORIAN!
I CAN'T TAKE IT ANYMORE!
I'M SICK OF THESE GUYS HURTING MY PEOPLE!
MY SISTER, MY QUEEN!
I CAN'T...!
I...!
THEY MIGHT HAVE EVEN KILLED NICO!
OUR PEOPLE, THEIR PEOPLE!
THERE'S NO SUCH THING!
IT DOESN'T HAVE TO EXIST!
DORIAN!
YOU STILL DON'T GET IT!

NO!

LEAVE HIM ALONE!

WHY ARE YOU SO CRUEL?

WE ONLY WANTED OUR QUEEN!

WE DON'T WANT TO GO BACK TO HOW IT WAS BEFORE...

BECAUSE OF HER...

WE COULD WALK THE STREETS WITHOUT ANY FEAR FOR THE FIRST TIME.

THANKS TO HER, WE STOPPED HIDING WHO WE ARE.

DANI...

YOU'RE SO SELFISH.

DANI, I...

I'VE FORGOTTEN SOMETHING IMPORTANT, HAVEN'T I?

WHAT IF WE COULD CHANGE IT?

WHAT IF WE COULD FIX IT ALL WITH OUR WILLPOWER?

WHAT WOULD YOU THINK OF ME NOW?

'CAUSE YOU NEVER DID ANYTHING WRONG.

NEVER.

I FEEL LIKE I'VE DISAPPOINTED YOU.

FOR JUST A SECOND, I'D LIKE TO STOP FEELING ANYTHING, ONCE AND FOR ALL.

ONCE AGAIN.

I THINK NICO...

...IS DYING.

WHA...?

BA-DUMP

BA-DUMP
NICO!
NO...
BA-DU
EVERYTHING SPILLED...
NICO, LOOK AT ME!
ARE YOU AWAKE?!
MMMH...
BA-DUMP
LET ME SEE...
AH!
HE'S LOSING A LOT OF BLOOD!
WHAT SHOULD WE DO...?
BA-DUMP
I'M FINE, I'M FINE.
DORIAN, LISTEN...
CAN YOU HEAL HIM WITH MAGIC, DORIAN?
NO...
I DON'T KNOW...
BA-DUMP

I'VE READ ABOUT HEALING SPELLS...
BUT I'VE NEVER PRACTICED THEM AND THEY'RE VERY HARD TO MAKE.
MONICA!
DO YOU HAVE A POTION FOR NICO?
N... NO...
MY POTIONS WERE ALL SMASHED EARLIER.
STOP IT, I'M FINE.
REALLY.
DORIAN...
YOU MUST LISTEN.
I KNOW WHAT HAPPENED TO DANI.
I HAVE NO IDEA HOW WE DIDN'T FIGURE THIS OUT EARLIER...
SHE CURSED HERSELF.
DANI...
WHAT?

EMOTIONLESS...
COMPLETELY EMOTIONLESS...
SHE...
SHE MUST HAVE SUFFERED A GREAT DEAL WHEN SHE SAW YOU DIE, DORIAN...
AND SHE WANTED TO ERASE THAT PAIN.
ERASING EVERYTHING ELSE ALONG WITH IT.
"THERE'S SOMETHING WAY MORE POWERFUL..." THAT MEANS...
THAT MEANS THAT IF DANI LOSES HER MAGICAL POWERS, THE CURSE WILL BE BROKEN?
AH...
MAY...
MAYBE.
DORIAN.
THIS IS THE POTION I USED ON YOUR MOTHER.
BUT...

DANI WOULD BE BACK...

WITHOUT HER POWERS, THOUGH.

PERHAPS THIS IS WHAT SHE WANTS. SHE WAS NEVER ENTIRELY HAPPY WITH THEM EITHER.

ALTHOUGH...

WHY DOES IT HURT SO MUCH TO THINK OF IT?

WHAT ELSE CAN WE DO?

DANI...

... ALL RIGHT.

COUGH

COUGH

COUGH

NICO!

WE NEED TO FIND SOMEONE WHO'S ABLE TO HEAL HIM.

THERE ARE MANY WITCHES, MAYBE SOMEONE CAN HELP.

NICO? ARE YOU THERE? SPEAK TO ME, SAY SOMETHING...

TELL MARK I CAN SMELL HIS ARMPITS...

THE VILLAGE IS A WRECK...

THEY HAVEN'T STOPPED FIGHTING... WITCHES AGAINST WITCHES.

THIS DOESN'T MAKE ANY SENSE.

WHAT ARE WE GONNA DO?

I DON'T KNOW...

THAT'S ENOUGH!

EVERYBODY.

STOP.

CAN'T YOU SEE WHAT YOU'RE DOING?!

YOU FIGHT FOR THE FREEDOM OF WITCHES...

BY ATTACKING OTHER WITCHES?!

IT'S OVER.

IT'S NOT OVER.

WE WANT OUR QUEEN.

LET'S MAKE A DEAL.

WE HEAL YOUR FRIEND.

YOU GIVE US OUR QUEEN AND ALLOW US TO LEAVE.

WE WON'T BOTHER YOU ANYMORE. WE'LL LEAVE AND LIVE OUR LIFE FAR AWAY.

WHERE NOBODY WILL LOCK US UP OR BURN US.

WE NEED THE QUEEN, THOUGH.

SHE'S OUR SYMBOL, THE LIGHT OF A TORCH THAT'LL GUIDE WHOEVER IS LOOKING FOR A BETTER PLACE.

WE WON'T ALLOW YOU TO LOCK HER UP.

DANIELA WYTTE IS MY SISTER. WE JUST WANT TO HEAL HER.

DO YOU THINK I'M BUYING THAT?
YOU MIGHT BE HER BROTHER, BUT YOU'RE A TRAITOR.
SHE WAS WITH MRS. WYTTE, NOT WITH YOU.
IT DOESN'T QUITE LOOK LIKE YOU'RE CLOSE EITHER.
BUT HEY, YOUR FRIEND NEEDS HELP.
DO YOU ACCEPT THE DEAL OR NOT?
...
LET MY SISTER GO...

WE NEED TO BE BETTER THAN THAT.

STOP BLABBERING!

DO YOU THINK I WEAR THIS 'CAUSE IT'S COOL?!

WELL, MAYBE JUST A LITTLE. IT LOOKS REALLY CUTE ON ME.

BUT IT'S ALSO MY SYMBOLIC GESTURE TOWARDS YOU.

TOWARDS EVERYONE!

WE AREN'T GONNA LOCK ANYBODY UP!

NOT THOSE WHO DO MAGIC AND NOT YOUR QUEEN.

YOU CAN REST ASSURED.

WE'RE ALL IN THE SAME BOAT.

THIS CLEARLY GOT A BIT OUT OF HAND.

SORRY IF I CAN'T ACTUALLY TRUST YOU...

YOUR FRIEND IS WOUNDED.

MINE TOO.

BUT I KNOW THAT NEITHER SIDE WAS AIMING TO KILL.

I'M ONLY ASKING FOR YOUR HELP.

I'VE SEEN YOU AIM AT OTHER PLACES, AT THE WALLS, TRYING TO INTIMIDATE US, BUT WITHOUT HURTING US.

PLEASE, WE CAN FIX THIS.

...

WELL...

MARTHA?

MARTHA!

WHAT ARE YOU DOING?

YOU'RE THE KING, AREN'T YOU?

DO YOU AGREE WITH EVERYTHING YOUR WIFE SAID?

DO YOU ALSO PROMISE YOU'RE GOING TO ENSURE THE SAFETY OF ALL WITCHES?

PROMISE ME NOBODY IN MY GROUP WILL END UP IN THE DUNGEONS.

WELL...

ALMOST NOBODY.

OF COURSE.

I SWEAR.

UH...

THANK YOU SO MUCH.

I'M GONNA TAKE THIS ONE WITH ME.
UNDERSTANDABLE.
NO PROBLEM. WE DIDN'T LIKE HIM ANYWAY.
THEY'RE WAITING FOR YOU...
KING WILLIAM.
AS YOU'VE JUST HEARD, THE WAR HAS COME TO AN END.
IT DOESN'T MAKE SENSE ANYMORE.
HOW MANY OF YOU WERE WITCHES BEFORE THIS WHOLE THING STARTED?

AND HOW MANY HAVE BECOME INTERESTED IN MAGIC OVER THE LAST COUPLE OF YEARS?

WE WERE ALL...

IDIOTS.

AND WHAT DOES IT MATTER, WHO STARTED FIRST AND WHO CAME LATER?

WE WERE ALL...

IDIOTS.

WE WERE ALL IDIOTS.

WE CAN CREATE SOMETHING NEW, THOUGH, ALL TOGETHER.

SOMETHING STRONGER AND BETTER.

WE'LL START BY RECONSTRUCTING THE VILLAGE,

JUST LIKE WE DID WITH THE MASTER'S HOUSE.

OH, THAT'S A GOOD IDEA!

MY HOUSE WAS TOTALLY SHATTERED!

WILL IT BE FREE?

THE FAÇADE OF MY HOUSE COULD REALLY USE A COAT OF PAINT.

IF YOU WANDER OFF, THE CYCLE WILL START AGAIN.

YOU DON'T NEED TO FEAR THE FUTURE.

I WAS ALSO SCARED.

BUT FEAR ISN'T FOREVER.

STAY HERE. SHARE.

MIX. COEXIST.

AND THEN PAST FEAR WON'T COME BACK.

NOT IF WE ALL STICK TOGETHER.

IT DOESN'T HAVE TO BE ALL BLACK AND GLOOMY.

HA-HA!

OH?

DORIAN?
WHAT?
WHAT DID MONICA SAY?
HUH?
YOU KNOW...
IT DOESN'T HAVE TO BE ALL BLACK AND GLOOMY.
WHOA!
WHY...?
WHOAAA!
WOW...

MY LATE FATHER-IN-LAW FORBADE PUNISHING WITCHES FOR DOING MAGIC.

IT WAS MANY YEARS AGO,

ALTHOUGH SOME PEOPLE LIKE MY FATHER DIDN'T RESPECT THAT RULE.

MONICA AND I, AS THE NEW QUEEN AND KING, ARE GOING TO TAKE A STEP FORWARD.

I DID ALL I COULD...

NOW HE NEEDS TO REST...

THANK YOU SO MUCH, REALLY.

AH...

OH... HOW LOVELY...

STARTING FROM NOW,

MAGIC WILL BE FOR EVERYONE.

DAMIEN...

I CAN SEE YOU MELTING.

SHUT UP!

HA-HA!

!

A WORLD IN WHICH MAGIC WILL BE FOR EVERYONE...

SOUNDS GOOD...

FOR EVERYONE EXCEPT FOR...

DID YOU DO THIS?!

DORIAN!

HOW COOL!
I THINK I WANT...
THIS ONE!
HE HE.
WHAT DO YOU THINK?
HOW DO I LOOK?

AH!
DO...
DORIAN...
NO WAY!
DANI...?
THE QUEEN...JUST CHANGED?
WHAT HAPPENED...?
DOES THIS MEAN THAT...
WE BROKE THE CURSE...?
SOMEHOW...?

AUGH...
SNIFF.
UGH...
WHY ARE YOU CRYING?
HEY...
YOU'RE GONNA MAKE ME CRY TOO.

CHAPTER 79

DORIAN...?

MMM?

IS IT REALLY YOU?

OF COURSE IT'S ME.

DANI?

BUT... I THINK I SAW YOU DIE...

YOU GOT BURNED.

I...

WAS IT A DREAM?

DID I MAKE IT ALL UP?

NO, YOU DIDN'T MAKE IT UP.

IT HAPPENED, BUT THAT WASN'T ME.

THIS IS REAL.

DANIII!

AH!

WE'VE MISSED YOU!

I'M SO GLAD YOU'RE BACK!

AW, I LOVE YOUR SMILE! YOU LOOK SO DIFFERENT NOW!

DAMIEN.
GO GIVE OUR SISTER A HUG.
COME ON.
NO.
HUUUH?
WHY NOT?!
COME ON, DON'T BE SHY!
I SAID NO!
SHE'LL THINK I'M WEIRD!
I'M GLAD YOU'RE OK!
THANK YOU, ANNE!
WAS I NOT DOING WELL?
ARGH!
DANI!
ARE YOU OK?
YES, I JUST TRIPPED OVER...
...MY HAIR?
WHAT...?
THIS HAIR IS STUPIDLY LONG.

AH! AND WHAT ABOUT THIS DRESS?!

I LOOK OLD!

NOW THAT YOU'RE NOT AN EVIL OVERLADY ANYMORE, IT DOESN'T SUIT YOU, TO BE HONEST.

SO YOU HAVE NO MEMORY AT ALL OF THE LAST THREE YEARS?

AH, HI DAMIEN.

I THINK...

...I DO?

I'M NOT SURE. I FEEL DIZZY...

AH...

WAIT.

NICO!

WELL, HE'S STILL UNCONSCIOUS.

HE HAS STOPPED BLEEDING THOUGH.

AH... MAJESTY.

WAIT.

DANI JUST WENT THROUGH A MAJOR SHOCK.

SHE NEEDS TO REST.

WE ALL DO.

LET'S TAKE SOME TIME TO REGAIN OUR STRENGTH.

WE WILL MEET LATER.

MY HUSBAND AND I HAVE AN OFFER FOR YOU.

THOSE WITCHES RECONSTRUCTED THE ROOFTOP IN JUST A FEW MINUTES.

AMAZING!

WITH THEIR HELP WE WILL FINISH IN NO TIME!

WE NEED MORE STONE. THESE FACADES ARE TOTALLY WRECKED.

WILL THERE BE ENOUGH MONEY?

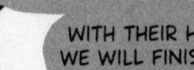

KING WILLIAM SAID HE'LL TAKE CARE OF THE EXPENSES.

IT TURNS OUT HE'S A GOOD GUY AFTER ALL.

HE HAS SOME GUTS, THAT'S FOR SURE!

WE WILL NEED LARGE BEAMS...
WOULD IT BE POSSIBLE TO ASSEMBLE SMALL PIECES OF BROKEN WOOD WITH MAGIC?
HEY.
AH, DAMIEN! I'M GLAD YOU'RE HERE!
CAN YOU HELP ME WITH THIS?
WHAT ARE YOU DOING IN THE BASEMENT?
I'M TRYING TO CALCULATE ALL THE MATERIALS WE NEED FOR THE RECONSTRUCTION OF THE VILLAGE.
BUT I HATE MATH!
THIS IS SO HARD, I SHOULD HAVE STUDIED MORE!
DON'T WORRY ABOUT MATH, WILL...
YOU'RE DOING GREAT.
REALLY, YOU HAD THE BEARING OF A TRUE KING TODAY.
AND I'M NOT JUST SAYING THIS BECAUSE I'M YOUR FRIEND!
EVERYONE THINKS SO.

TODAY YOU WERE THE MOST AMAZING PERSON I'VE EVER SEEN.
AND, WELL, I...
UH...
THAT'S IT.
WE SHOULD GO TO THE MEETING WITH MONICA AND THE WITCHES.
WAIT, DAMIEN!
I...
YOU...
MAYBE YOU WERE RIGHT.
I MIGHT BE ABLE TO WEAR THE CROWN PROUDLY AND DO A GOOD JOB.
MAYBE IT'S TRUE THAT I CAN BE WORTHY ENOUGH.
AND MOST IMPORTANTLY,

I MAY NOT HAVE TO DENY WHAT I AM IN ORDER TO DO MY DUTY.
WHAT--?
UH...
WHAT ARE YOU DOING, WILL?!
COME ON, THIS WASN'T EVEN THE FIRST ONE.

SO YOU KNEW AND DECIDED TO PLAY DUMB?!
YES, I KNOW YOU GAVE ME A KISS OF TRUE LOVE AND WOKE ME UP!
WHY ARE YOU LEAVING, ARE YOU EMBARRASSED?!
STOP MAKING FUN OF ME.
WHAT DO YOU WANT?
I'VE ALREADY TOLD YOU.
I WANT TO TRY IT.
I WANT TO BE A GOOD KING AND AT THE SAME TIME LISTEN TO WHAT I FEEL.
SO YOU KISSED ME BECAUSE...
THAT'S RIGHT.
JUST BECAUSE I FELT LIKE IT.
YOU IDIOT!

NICO!
YOU FINALLY WOKE UP!
POW
GUUUYS, NICO IS AWAKE!

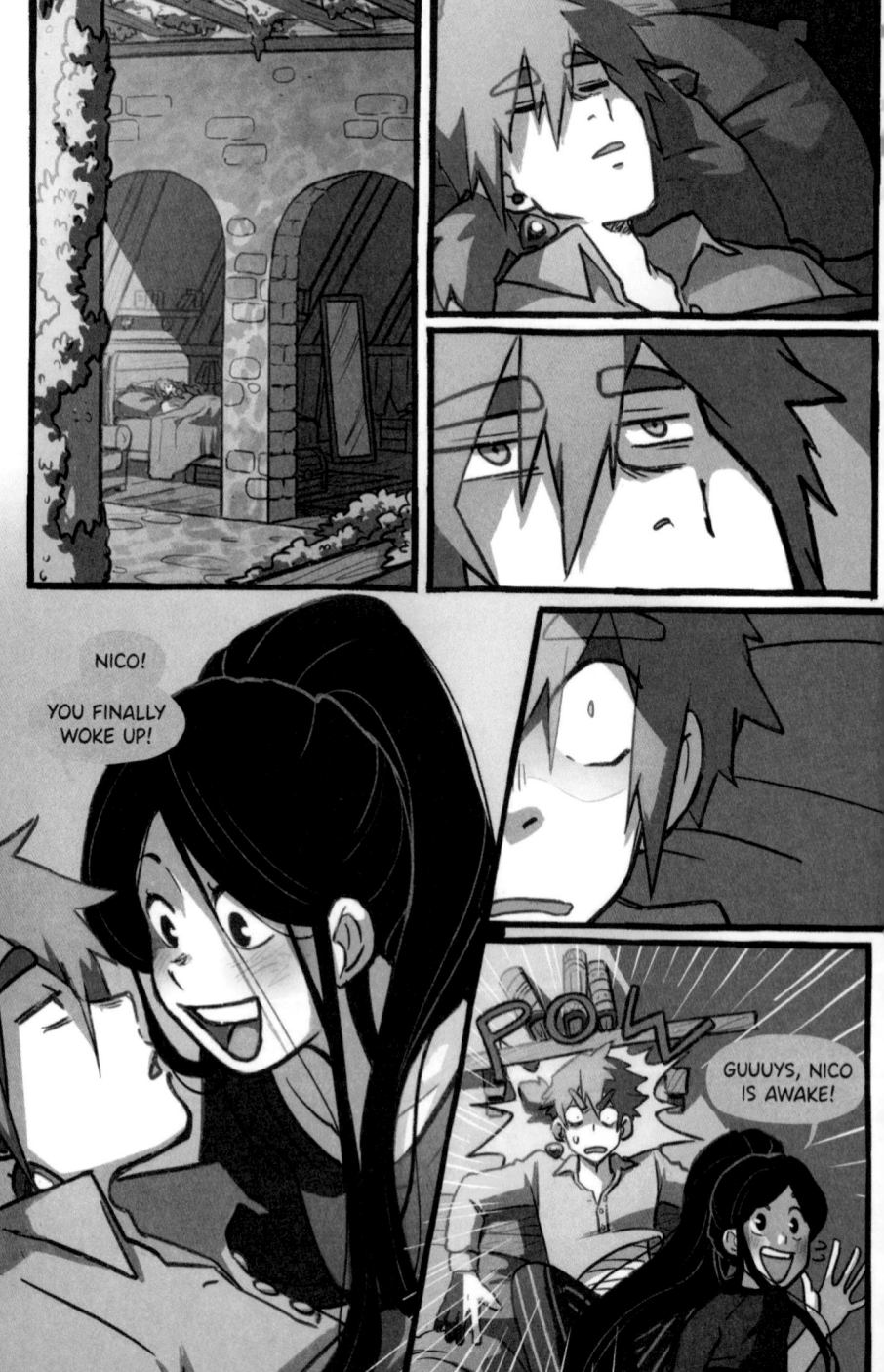

UH...
A... ARE YOU OK?
HEY...
NICO...?
IS THIS REALLY YOU?
IT'S NOT A DREAM, IS IT?
AH?
NO!
IT'S ME!
I WANTED TO THANK YOU...
HANG ON.
JUST A SECOND.
I NEED TO PROCESS IT.
I CAN'T BELIEVE I'M TALKING TO YOU...
AND THAT YOU'RE ANSWERING BACK...

I'M SORRY FOR NOT ANSWERING UNTIL NOW.

I WANTED TO THANK YOU FOR BEING BY MY SIDE, NICO.

FOR NOT LEAVING ME ALONE EVEN THOUGH...

MAYBE I DESERVED IT.

YOU WEREN'T DOING WELL.

I WASN'T GOING TO ABANDON YOU BECAUSE OF THAT.

YOU REMEMBER EVERYTHING, THEN?

WELL...

IT'S WEIRD, A BIT LIKE A DREAM.

GLIMPSES OF FOGGY MEMORIES ARE COMING TO ME, MORE AND MORE.

...

WHAT?

I'M SORRY.

I'M JUST REALLY NERVOUS. I STILL CAN'T BELIEVE IT.

NICO...

HOW WAS THE CURSE BROKEN?

IT HAPPENED WHEN WILLIAM AND MONICA WERE TALKING TO THE PEOPLE.

THEY WERE PROMISING THEM A BETTER FUTURE.

DORIAN MADE A LOT OF COLORFUL HATS FLY,

IT WAS BEAUTIFUL...

AND SUDDENLY I FELT AS IF...

AS IF I HAD BEEN LOCKED INSIDE A SMALL ROOM,

DARK AND DUSTY,

AND THEN A DOOR OPENED,

BATHING EVERYTHING WITH LIGHT.

IT WAS LIKE...

...GETTING OUT OF A PRISON CELL.

I FIGURED IT...

IT WASN'T JUST DORIAN'S "DEATH", WAS IT?

WHAT HURT YOU, WHAT MADE YOU WANT TO DISAPPEAR.

IT WAS ALSO ALEX, YOUR DAD,

ALL THE TIMES YOU'VE FELT TRAPPED BETWEEN TWO SIDES IN A TERRIBLE CONFLICT.

YES, YOU'RE RIGHT.

NICO, YOU GOT SO SMART.

I'M NOT SMART.

THIS IS ALL I COULD COME UP WITH IN THREE YEARS.

AND EVEN THEN, IT TOOK ME A WHILE TO REALIZE IT.

NICOOO! YOU'VE SCARED US A LOT!

HEY!

I'M SORRY!

HOW ARE YOU FEELING?

PERFECTLY WELL!

DID YOU SEE?

YES, SHE'S BACK WITH US.

OUCH!

WHAT ON EARTH ARE YOU WEARING, DANI?

AH! I BORROWED IT FROM MARK.

AH! HE BEAT ME TO IT!

MARK, WAIT 'TIL I CATCH YOU...

OF COURSE, MUFFIN BOY.

REGARDLESS, I CAN'T ALLOW YOU TO WEAR THAT.

LUCKILY, YOUR DEAR MONICA IS HERE!

COME, COME, LET'S TRY SOME DRESSES ON.

AH, WAIT...!

NICO, I'M JUST TAKING HER FOR A WHILE.

YOU EXPERIENCED TOO MANY STRONG EMOTIONS IN A SINGLE DAY, AND YOU'RE WOUNDED.

LET YOUR HEART REST FOR A BIT.

...

OHHH, DANI, I'M SO GLAD YOU'RE HERE!

WHOA, SO MANY PEOPLE CAME.
EVEN FROM ANOTHER TOWN, IT SEEMS.
I HOPE IT'LL BE FINE.
I HOPE SO TOO...
DON'T WORRY, GUYS...
THIS TIME AROUND, I'M TAKING A QUEEN WITH ME.
AS SOON AS THEY SEE DANI, THEY'LL LISTEN.
I THINK I'M GONNA FAINT.
CHEER UP, DANI!
YOU LOOK STUNNING.
THANK YOU, GIRLS.
THIS IS SO INTERESTING, MONICA...
IN MY KINGDOM, WE HAVEN'T EXPERIENCED ANY DISCRIMINATION BETWEEN WITCHES AND NON-WITCHES IN A LONG TIME, BUT STILL...
YES, I LIKE IT.
YOU DID A GREAT JOB.
THANKS!
I DID IT WITH DORIAN AND DAMIEN. WE ALL SHARE THE CREDIT.
COULD YOU BY ANY CHANCE SEND AN EMISSARY TO MY PALACE?
I'D LIKE TO IMPLEMENT THIS PROJECT.

CHAPTER 80

SERIOUSLY?

CONSIDER IT DONE!

HEY, DANI.

ARE YOU READY?

DORIAN...!

HEY, WE'RE MATCHING!

I KNOW!

IT COULDN'T BE ANY OTHER WAY.

WE WILL MAKE AN IMPECCABLE IMPRESSION ON THE PEOPLE.

HOW ARE YOU FEELING? NERVOUS?

I NEED TO CONVINCE ALL THOSE PEOPLE NOT TO KILL MONICA, AND THEREUPON ABDICATE IN HER FAVOR.

INCREDIBLY.

DON'T WORRY.

IF I SEE YOU STRUGGLE, I'LL BE THERE TO CHANGE A FEW HAT COLORS HERE AND THERE!

THANK YOU SO MUCH, DORIAN!

JUST THINK THAT AFTER THIS, YOU WON'T BE THE QUEEN ANYMORE.

YOU WILL BE FREE TO MAKE YOUR OWN DECISIONS.

MY DECISIONS...?

HOW ABOUT YOU, DORIAN?

DANI, HURRY UP,

YOU NEED TO GO OUT AT THE SAME TIME AS MONICA!

HAVE YOU DECIDED WHAT YOU WANT TO DO?

YES, I'VE MADE UP MY MIND.

COME ON, DANI. THEY'RE WAITING FOR YOU.

GET READY AS WELL, DORIAN.

...

THANK YOU ALL SO MUCH FOR COMING HERE TODAY.

WE HAVE A BIG ANNOUNCEMENT TO MAKE.

SOMETHING THAT WILL CHANGE THE WORLD FOREVER.

RUN, JULIA!

WE'RE GONNA MISS THE BUS!

JUST DON'T RUN SO FAST!

OH NO, IT'S LEAVING ALREADY!

I CAN ONLY COME UP WITH ONE THING.

WAAAIT!

HURRY UP, GET ON THE BROOM.

WAIT, KIDS...

THAT'S DANGEROUS...

OH!

WHOA!

AWESOME!

SC REEEH

HEY, YOU! WHAT DO YOU THINK YOU'RE DOING?

THAT WAS DANGEROUS!

THANK YOU FOR STOPPING!

THANKS!

WE COULDN'T MISS THE FIRST DAY OF CLASS!

YEAH, BUT YOU DIDN'T NEED TO GO SO FAST ON THAT BROOM...

IT'S NOT LIKE THE SCHOOL IS HIDDEN.

GOOD MORNING, EVERYONE.

AS YOU KNOW, THIS COURSE IS PART OF A GREAT EDUCATIONAL REFORM.

HOW HANDSOME...

I HOPE HE'S GONNA BE OUR NEW TUTOR...

STARTING NOW, A NUMBER OF SUBJECTS WILL BE ADDED,

INCLUDING POTION-MAKING, FLYING ON A BROOM,

ELEMENTAL SPELLS, DOMESTIC SPELLS, DIVINATION, AND SO FORTH...

LET'S START QUEEN MONICA'S NEW MAGIC SCHOOL PROJECT!

Dorian Wytte

I'M PROFESSOR WYTTE, AND I'LL BE YOUR ELEMENTAL SPELLS TEACHER.

DO YOU HAVE ANY QUESTIONS?

CAN WE WEAR A POINTY HAT?

NOT IN CLASS. YOU'D MAKE IT HARD FOR YOUR CLASSMATES TO SEE PROPERLY.

ARE WE STILL GONNA STUDY MATH?

Dorian Wytte

OF COURSE. ALL SUBJECTS MATTER!

HOW DISAPPOINTING...

PROFESSOR, DO YOU HAVE A GIRLFRIEND?

WHAT?!

WHY...?! THAT'S NOT...!

DORIAAAN!

SORRY FOR BEING SO LATE!

HOW WAS YOUR DAY?

AH. WHAT ARE YOU UP TO? STILL READING?

YES... I WANTED TO PROPERLY REVIEW TOMORROW'S CLASS.

IT'LL BE CRUCIAL, YOU KNOW?

WE'RE GONNA GIVE STUDENTS THEIR FIRST TEST.

YOU'VE WORKED ENOUGH FOR TODAY.

OH!

CAKE?!

HE HE, TONIGHT WE'LL HAVE CAKE FOR DINNER.

MARK GAVE IT TO ME, FOR YOU.

WE SHOULD EAT CAKE EVERY DAY.

AND NOW, WE'LL LEAVE YOU TO SOME MUSICAL MOMENTS.

DORIAN... I SAW DAMIEN TODAY.

HOW DID IT GO? DID YOU TALK?

HE ASKED ME...

IF WE'RE READY TO GO AND SEE MUM.

...

... YES.

WE SHOULD GO.

DAMIEN!

GOOD MORNING.

YOU'RE LATE.

SORRY TO KEEP YOU WAITING.

WOW! WHAT'S WITH THE OUTFIT?

DID YOU DRESS UP LIKE THAT FOR MUM?

SHUT UP.

...

WHAT HAPPENED WITH THE PRISONERS OF WAR, DAMIEN?

THOSE WHO DID NOT COMMIT VIOLENT CRIMES WON'T RECEIVE ANY CHARGES.

AS FOR THE OTHERS, WELL...

MOST OF THEM HAVE BEEN DEPORTED AND DEPRIVED OF THEIR MAGICAL POWERS.

AUNT HILDE SAID THAT SHE DIDN'T CARE IF SHE LOST HER MAGIC,

BUT STILL, SINCE SHE WAS ONE OF THE LEADERS, SHE HAD TO PAY A LARGE SUM OF MONEY AS COMPENSATION.

THOSE FUNDS WILL GO DIRECTLY TO THE SCHOOL.

AUNT HILDE...

AND WHERE IS SHE NOW?

POOR THING, SHE REALLY LOVED HER MONEY.

I HEARD THAT SHE SET UP A POTION BUSINESS IN THE OUTSKIRTS OF THE KINGDOM.

IT'S GOING PRETTY WELL.

UM...

WHAT ABOUT THE MASTER?

IS HE STILL IN JAIL?

PENDRAGON...

HE WAS BROKE, BUT HE WAS DEPRIVED OF HIS POWERS AND DEPORTED.

HE LEFT SILENTLY, WITH HIS HEAD LOW.

WE HAVEN'T HEARD ABOUT HIM EVER SINCE.

I DON'T THINK...

WE'LL EVER SEE HIM AGAIN.

AND THEN THERE'S HER,

ANGELA WYTTE.

MUM.

HELLO, MUM.

GOOD MORNING!

YOU'RE A BIT LATE TODAY!

DAMIEN!

I KNOW, I'M SORRY.

I HAD SOMETHING TO DO.

HAVE YOU ALREADY HAD BREAKFAST, SWEETHEART?

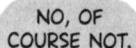

NO, OF COURSE NOT.

WE'RE GONNA HAVE BREAKFAST TOGETHER AS ALWAYS, RIGHT?

AH...

OH, WELL, I HAVE ALREADY EATEN! I'M SORRY!

OH, COME ON...!

...

HI, MUM.

DORIAN... DANI...

MUM!

YOU CAME...

I'M GLAD TO SEE YOU'RE FINE.

DANI, SWEETHEART...

WHAT HAPPENED?

I DON'T KNOW.

BUT EVERYTHING'S OKAY NOW.

...

MUM, DANI AND I ARE LIVING TOGETHER CLOSE BY.

I THOUGHT YOU COULD ALSO SETTLE...

DORIAN.

MUM IS GONNA LIVE HERE WITH ME, AT THE PALACE.

SHE'LL BE FINE. THERE'S NOTHING TO WORRY ABOUT.

SHE WON'T BE LOCKED UP.

IT'S NOT A PROBLEM FOR ME AT ALL.

SHE'S MY MOTHER.

AND ALSO MINE.

I'VE ALLOWED YOU TO TAKE ALL THE RESPONSIBILITY FOR WAY TOO LONG.

YOU NEED TO GET ON WITH YOUR LIVES. YOU'RE STILL KIDS.

LET ME DO THIS.

MOREOVER, I LIKE HAVING HER HERE.

COME ON,

GIVE HER A HUG.

SHE SAYS SHE HAS NOWHERE TO GO,

BECAUSE IT DOESN'T MAKE SENSE TO BE SEPARATED FROM HER KIDS.

PERHAPS, LITTLE BY LITTLE, OVER TIME...

WE'LL MANAGE TO BE A FAMILY AGAIN.

CHAPTER 81

I'M OFF TO SCHOOL, DANI.
WHAT ARE YOU UP TO TODAY?
AH? WELL, I SUPPOSE...
NOTHING.
I'LL CRASH ON THE SOFA.
COME ON, DON'T SAY THAT.
WHEN I'M BACK, WE COULD GO FOR A NOCTURNAL PICNIC.
BYE!
...
SOUNDS GOOD...
BUT...
BUT I CAN'T GO ON LIKE THIS.
DORIAN, MONICA, DAMIEN, WILLIAM, MARK, EVEN NICO...
EVERYONE ELSE IS MAKING DECISIONS, LIVING THEIR LIVES, AND DOING GREAT AND KIND THINGS.
WHAT CAN I DO, THOUGH?
I NEED TO STOP BEING LAZY AND MAKE UP MY MIND!
I GOT IT!
ONLY ONE PLACE CAN HELP ME FIGURE OUT MY FUTURE!

THAT'S ALL FOR TODAY!

SEE YOU TOMORROW, PROFESSOR WYTTE!

HI, PROFESSOR WYTTE!

ARE YOU FREE TO GO ON A DATE WITH ME YET?

MONICA!

WHAT ARE YOU DOING HERE?!

IF THE CHILDREN DISCOVER US, IT WILL BE A DISASTER!

SO YOU'RE ENJOYING YOUR LIFE AS A TEACHER?

I LOVE IT!

SEEING THE CHILDREN'S PROGRESS IN MAGIC IS WONDERFUL.

AND I SPEND MOST OF MY TIME READING!

I'M BUILDING MY DREAM LIBRARY AT HOME!

I'LL BORROW YOUR FAVORITE NOVELS, THEN!

I DON'T HAVE ANY...

I THINK NOVELS ARE A WASTE OF TIME. YOU CAN'T LEARN ANYTHING FROM THEM.

ARE YOU KIDDING?!

READ SOME OF THEM, YOU WON'T REGRET IT!

THEY'VE INSPIRED ME AND MADE ME GROW!

I'LL READ THEM ALL.

IN NOVELS YOU CAN LEARN ABOUT LIFE, ABOUT THE VERY ESSENCE OF HUMAN BEINGS!

WHAT?!

I LOVE HOW PASSIONATE YOU ARE ABOUT IT.

I WANT US TO EXPERIENCE TOGETHER THE THINGS THAT MAKE YOU HAPPY!

DORIAN...

AH!

I'M EXPERIENCING A SECRET, FORBIDDEN LOVE STORY.

HOW EXCITING!

DO YOU THINK I'M THE WORST FOR ENJOYING THIS SO MUCH?

I THINK YOU READ TOO MANY NOVELS.

HA-HA!

THE ALLEY OF THE FUTURE
CLAIRVOYANTS AND FORTUNE-TELLERS FOR ALL BUDGETS.
HELLO, CAN I COME IN?
YES, COME ON IN...
WHAT DO YOU WANNA KN...?
AH.
IT'S YOU, DANI!
I'LL NEED TO USE MY POWERS FOR REAL NOW.
DON'T YOU DO THAT FOR YOUR CLIENTS?!
WHY WOULD I?
I DRAW THE CARDS, MAKE UP SOMETHING FOOLISH, AND GET THE CASH.
ZERO COMPLICATIONS.
YOU WOULDN'T BELIEVE HOW GOOD I AM AT IMPROVISING!
WOW, HOW COOL!
I WANT YOU TO GIVE ME A READING!
ALL RIGHT, SO, WHAT'S YOUR QUESTION?
WHAT'S ON YOUR MIND?

DANI...ARE YOU WORRIED ABOUT SOMETHING?

...

NO, WELL...

I'VE BEEN THINKING ABOUT IT FOR SOME TIME.

BEFORE, MY GOAL WAS TO SAVE THE WORLD, BUT... WHAT NOW?

WHAT AM I SUPPOSED TO DO?

YOU MEAN YOU WANNA LOOK FOR A JOB? IS THAT IT?

BECAUSE YOU COULD...

NO, NO.

DORIAN HAS ALREADY TOLD ME LOTS OF JOB IDEAS.

I NEED...

SOMETHING ELSE. I NEED TO FIND MY PLACE.

HOW SILLY, YOUR PLACE IS WITH M...

WITH US!

WITH YOUR FRIENDS, THOSE WHO CARE ABOUT YOU!

YEAH, BUT THOSE I CARE ABOUT ARE DOING SOMETHING USEFUL AND IMPORTANT.

I...HAVE NOTHING TO DO.

ALL RIGHT.

I'M GONNA GIVE YOU A READING.

YAY!

I ROUGHLY KNOW THE MEANING, BUT THEY'RE NOTHING MORE THAN ARCHETYPES AND...

ARE YOU PAYING ATTENTION?

WHAT DOES THE FOOL MEAN?!

IT COULD POSSIBLY INDICATE A TRIP OR...?

UM...

IT STANDS FOR SOMETHING LIKE...

A FREE SPIRIT, INNOCENCE, THE START OF SOMETHING NEW...

NICO, YOU'VE ENLIGHTENED ME!

WHAT? THIS FAST?

THIS CARD REPRESENTS A JOURNEY...

AND LOOK, THERE'S A SUN IN THE PICTURE!

THE LIGHT OF A TORCH THAT'LL GUIDE WHOEVER IS LOOKING FOR A BETTER PLACE.

THAT'S ME!

DANI, YOU'RE THE IDEAL CLIENT OF ANY SCAM TAROT-READER.

NO, LISTEN!

THAT'S MY MISSION, TO FINISH WHAT I STARTED WHEN I WAS UNDER THE SPELL!

I HAVE TO VISIT OTHER KINGDOMS AND BRING THEM MONICA'S VISION FOR A SCHOOL OF FREE MAGIC FOR EVERYONE.
TO PREVENT BAD THINGS FROM HAPPENING AGAIN IN THE FUTURE.
YOU MEAN YOU WANT TO...
LEAVE?
NO, NO...
WELL, JUST A LITTLE.
BUT I'M PRETTY FAST WITH THE BROOM.
PERHAPS I'LL BE GONE FOR A FEW WEEKS FROM TIME TO TIME.
EH, NICO...
NO, IT'S OKAY...
IT'S JUST THAT IT MAKES ME SAD.
YOU'VE BEEN COMING HERE EVERY DAY LATELY.
I JUST CAN'T REMAIN UNEMPLOYED FOREVER.
...
RIGHT...
UH...
LISTEN, DANI... I...
THERE'S SOMETHING...
I MUST TELL YOU.

WELL, I'VE ACTUALLY ALREADY TOLD YOU...
MAYBE YOU DON'T REMEMBER, BUT...
THE TRUTH IS I...
I'VE ALWAYS...
WAIT!
DON'T...
DON'T SAY IT JUST YET.
DO YOU KNOW WHAT I'M ABOUT TO SAY?
OH...
YOU KNOW WHAT I'M ABOUT TO SAY.

RIGHT NOW I'M TRYING TO FIGURE OUT WHAT MY PLACE IS IN LIFE.
I NEED... A LITTLE BIT OF...
...TIME.
AH, OF COURSE...
I UNDERSTAND.
I'VE BEEN CLOSE TO YOU FOR THREE YEARS!
OF COURSE, I CAN GIVE YOU SOME SPACE!
NO, IT'S NOT THAT...
I DON'T WANT TO GET AWAY FROM YOU...
NICO...
COME WITH ME.
WHAT?
COME SPREAD THE MESSAGE THROUGHOUT THE WORLD WITH ME!

DO YOU REALLY MEAN IT?
I...
YES. I REALLY WANNA GO.
OF COURSE! YOU SAID YOU'D BE HAPPY DOING ANYTHING!
IT'LL BE FUN!
ALSO, MANY HERE HAVE DISCOVERED MY SCAM.
I NEED TO LOOK FOR NEW VICTIMS!
YOU MEAN CLIENTS.
WHATEVER.
I WANT YOU BY MY SIDE, NICO.
OH.
RIGHT NOW I'M CONFUSED.
BUT ONE THING I KNOW IS...

DO YOU ALREADY KNOW EVERYTHING BY HEART, DANI?

YES!

WELL, MORE OR LESS.

I'LL STUDY ON THE WAY. I PROMISE!

JUST IN CASE YOU FORGET SOMETHING, YOU'VE GOT MY SIGNED REPORTS.

ALTHOUGH, ANYONE WOULD WANT TO STUDY MAGIC JUST BY LOOKING AT THAT ADORABLE OUTFIT.

YOU'RE THE BEST MESSENGER I COULD WISH FOR!

AND YOU DIDN'T ORDER A UNIFORM FOR NICO, MONICA?

I WON'T BE WORKING AS A MESSENGER!

I WANTED TO SEE IT.

I'M ONLY GOING WITH DANI TO EARN SOME CASH FROM UNWISE NEW CLIENTS.

YEAH, I'M SURE THAT'S THE MAIN REASON WHY YOU'RE GOING WITH HER...

AH! HELLO WILLIAM. HI DAMIEN!

SEE? SHE HASN'T LEFT YET!

I TOLD YOU!

DAMIEN WAS AFRAID YOU LEFT BEFORE HE COULD SAY GOODBYE, DANI.

HUH?

REALLY?

DON'T WORRY, I'M ONLY GONNA BE GONE FOR A FEW WEEKS!

YEAH, BUT IT'S YOUR FIRST TRIP ON YOUR OWN AS A MESSENGER...

I THOUGHT I COULD GIVE YOU SOME ADVICE, PERHAPS... AS YOUR OLDER BROTHER...

I'M NOT GOING ON MY OWN!

NICO IS COMING WITH ME.

HEY!

...

THEN I'M GONNA GIVE A PIECE OF ADVICE TO YOU INSTEAD...

HEY, YOU'RE FREAKING ME OUT!

WELL, LET'S NOT WASTE ANY TIME.
ARE YOU NERVOUS, DANI?
A BIT, BUT I'M EXCITED!
DO YOU HAVE ENOUGH FOOD FOR THE TRIP?
DO YOU WANT SOME PUDDING?
NO THANKS, MARK!
BUNDLE UP!
IT'S COLD UP THERE IN THE SKY.
YES! DON'T WORRY, DAMIEN.
YOU'LL DO A GREAT JOB.
I'M SURE OF IT.
THANK YOU, DORIAN!
I HOPE I'LL BE GOOD ENOUGH.
OF COURSE YOU WILL.
AS SOON AS YOU APPEAR, PIROUETTING IN THE SKY,
EVERYONE IS GONNA WANT TO BE LIKE DANI THE WITCH.
AND LATER THEY'LL NEED TO DEAL WITH PROFESSORS LIKE ME.
I'M NOT VERY CHARMING, BUT RATHER IMPLACABLE!
BETWEEN THE TWO OF US, WE'LL MAKE GREAT WITCHES OUT OF THEM!
YES, WE'RE A GOOD TEAM.

...
I'LL MISS YOU LOTS!
BE CAREFUL!
I ASKED CARLO TO WATCH OVER YOU!
I'LL BE HOME WAITING FOR YOU!
DORIAAAAN!
I WON'T BE GONE FOR TOO LONG!
DON'T CRY, YOU'RE MAKING ME CRY TOO!
GOODBYE FOLKS!
SEE YA!
SEE YOU SOON!
WE LOVE YOU GUYS!
GOOD LUCK!
BYE!

YES, I'M SURE OF IT.

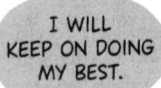

I WILL KEEP ON DOING MY BEST.

WE ALL WILL.

WE WILL WORK TOGETHER

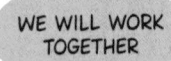

WITH WHAT WE HAVE, WITH EVERYTHING WE HAVE LEARNED.

SO THAT, LITTLE BY LITTLE,

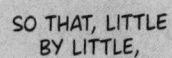

WE WILL BE ABLE TO RECTIFY PAST MISTAKES,

AND CREATE A BETTER WORLD FOR EVERYONE.

THE END

•EPILOGUE•

TELL ME, MY DEAR CHILDREN...

HOW ARE YOUR LOVE LIVES GOING?

COME ON, DON'T BE SHY!

TELL YOUR MOM ABOUT YOUR BOYFRIENDS AND GIRLFRIENDS!

I'M SINGLE.

OF COURSE, YOU'RE STILL VERY YOUNG, DANI.

AND SO IS DORIAN.

BUT MY DAMIEN HAS ALREADY REACHED MARRIAGEABLE AGE.

TELL ME, SWEETHEART, IS THERE A GIRL WHO HAS STOLEN YOUR HEART?

HOW AM I SUPPOSED TO TELL HER?

NO, THERE'S NO GIRL...

PERFECT, BECAUSE I'VE BEEN THINKING...

SINCE WE'RE NOW FOLLOWING THIS "PEACEFUL" ROUTE AND YOU THREE HAVE CONNECTIONS TO ROYALTY...

YOU, DAMIEN, COULD SEDUCE MONICA.

THEN DANI COULD SEDUCE KING WILLIAM...

...AND WE, THE WYTTES, WILL GET ALL THE POWER OF THE CROWN.

IT'S AN EXCELLENT PLAN...

OH, IT'S FUNNY YOU SHOULD MENTION THAT, MOM...

ACTUALLY, WE HAVE A SLIGHTLY DIFFERENT SUGGESTION.

FARMERS KEEP COMPLAINING THAT SOME FIELDS ARE STILL BARREN BECAUSE OF THE MAGIC WARS.

AHA...

I SUGGEST THAT MONICA SET UP RESEARCH IN HER POTIONS LAB TO FIND SOMETHING THAT CAN RETURN FERTILITY TO THE LAND.

SOUNDS GOOD.

HOWEVER, THERE IS SOMETHING IMPORTANT I WOULD LIKE TO CONSULT YOU ON, DAMIEN...

WHAT?

I WOULD LIKE TO REWARD YOUR LOYALTY AS A ROYAL ADVISER BY TAKING YOU TO DINNER.

WHAT DO YOU SAY?

WILL!

I MEAN...YOUR MAJESTY!

OF COURSE I ACCEPT YOUR HONORABLE REWARD.

DO THOSE TWO EVEN TRY TO HIDE ANYTHING ANYMORE?

POOR QUEEN MONICA, WHAT A HUSBAND...

I HEARD THAT SHE ALSO HAS A WITCH BOY AS A VERY GOOD FRIEND.

393

AH, THERE YOU ARE!

MONICA TOLD ME YOU WANTED TO SEE ME!

YES... I NEED TO TALK TO YOU...

HA HA HA

WHAT ARE YOU DOING WITH YOUR SHIRT ALL BUTTONED UP?

I DON'T KNOW, MONICA SAID IT LOOKS BETTER LIKE THIS.

TO CONQUER A GIRL'S HEART, YOU HAVE TO BE CLASSY AND CHIVALROUS!

BUTTON UP YOUR SHIRT, NICO!

AND GOOD LUCK!

MONICA HAS NO IDEA!

IT DOESN'T SUIT YOU.

AH!

DANI, I...

THE TRUTH IS THAT I WANTED TO TELL YOU...

SEE? MUCH BETTER.

...THAT I...

CUTE GUYS LOOK BETTER IN CASUAL CLOTHES.

WHAT?! WHAT DID YOU JUST SAY?!

AH!

NOTHING! I DIDN'T SAY ANYTHING AT ALL, FORGET IT!

DANI, WAIT! DON'T LEAVE!

EPILOGUE 4

THE QUEEN GETS ALONG *REALLY* WELL WITH THAT WITCH BOY. RIGHT, YOUR MAJESTY?

HUH?

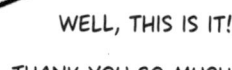

WELL, THIS IS IT!

THANK YOU SO MUCH FOR READING THIS FAR. I HOPE YOU ENJOYED READING *HOOKY* AS MUCH AS I ENJOYED WRITING IT.

I STARTED CREATING THIS STORY ALMOST BY CHANCE IN 2015, AS MANY OF YOU KNOW, ON THE WEBTOON PLATFORM.

AND IN EARLY 2020 I FINISHED DRAWING THE ADVENTURES OF DANI AND DORIAN. AT THE TIME I'D ALREADY SAID GOODBYE TO THEM (AND TO THE READERS!), AND I DIDN'T THINK THAT THREE YEARS LATER I WOULD BE SAYING GOODBYE TO THEM AGAIN AND PROBABLY FOR GOOD.

THE TRUTH IS THAT I STILL FIND IT HARD TO BELIEVE!

HOOKY HAS BEEN WITH ME FOR EIGHT YEARS OF MY LIFE! IT HAS MEANT A LOT OF WORK AND DEDICATION. FIRST, IN WEBTOON, I WROTE AND DREW ONE EPISODE PER WEEK. THE TRUTH IS THAT THE DEADLINES SOMETIMES WERE A STRUGGLE FOR ME. THEN, I HAD TO TRANSLATE THE WHOLE STORY INTO THE LANGUAGE OF TRADITIONAL COMICS. THIS MEANT DOING A REVISION AND REORGANIZATION OF ABSOLUTELY EVERYTHING.

BUT IT WAS WORTH EVERY MINUTE OF IT. TO BE ABLE TO SHARE MY STORIES WITH THE WORLD AND SEE THAT ON THE OTHER SIDE, OTHERS ENJOY THEM WITH THE SAME INTENSITY AS I DO, IS SOMETHING ABSOLUTELY WONDERFUL.

THANK YOU SO MUCH FOR YOUR SUPPORT. TRULY.

FOR EVERY COMMENT ON WEBTOON AND ON MY SOCIAL MEDIA, FOR EVERY VIDEO EDIT, FOR EVERY FANART, FOR EVERY TIME YOU CAME TO THE SIGNINGS AND TOLD ME HOW MUCH YOU LIKED THE STORY, OR HOW MUCH YOU LOVED THIS OR THAT CHARACTER. I'M DELIGHTED WHEN YOU TELL ME THAT MY STORY HAS ENCOURAGED YOU TO CREATE YOUR OWN, OR WHEN YOU CONFESS THAT MY COMIC WAS THE ONE THAT MADE YOU FALL IN LOVE WITH READING.

YOU ALL MAKE IT ALL MAKE SENSE.

DANI, DORIAN, AND THE WHOLE GANG WILL ALWAYS HAVE A VERY SPECIAL PLACE IN MY HEART. THEY ARE MY KIDS! I'VE GROWN UP WITH THEM, BOTH AS A PERSON AND AS AN ARTIST. BUT NOW IT'S TIME TO SAY GOODBYE. I'M GOING TO MISS THEM A LOT.

(ALTHOUGH, TO BE HONEST, I DON'T THINK I'LL BE ABLE TO AVOID DRAWING THEM FROM TIME TO TIME!)

THANKS FOR EVERYTHING,

MÍRIAM BONASTRE TUR
2023